Anyone U Want

CW00468749

A BBW, Scifi, BDSM, Billionaire novella

Evangeline Anderson

* * * * *

PUBLISHED BY:

Evangeline Anderson Books

Anyone U want

Copyright © 2016 by Evangeline Anderson

Please note all person portrayed are 18 years of age or older.

Author's Note: To be the first to hear about new e-book releases, join my new 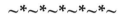newsletter. I promise no spam — you will only get email from me when a new book is out for either preorder or for sale.

~*~*~*~*~*~

Chapter One

"Five minutes until your meeting, Mr. Harris. The board is all assembled and waiting for you." Holly Sparks nodded at the antique grandfather clock in the corner of her boss's office which cost more than her car. A lot more. Grant Harris the Third was a meticulously punctual man and he hated to be late anywhere. Keeping him on time and up-to-date on the details of his many meetings was part of her job as his personal assistant.

"Very well, thank you, Miss Sparks." Mr. Harris always spoke formally, his tone clipped and with a hint of a British accent. He stood up from behind the massive oak desk that had belonged to his grandfather and straightened his tie. "I'm ready. How do I look?"

Words rose to the tip of Holly's tongue but she swallowed them down hastily. How did he look? In a word, luscious. Dark, dangerous, and delicious. Perfect. And completely unattainable.

At six-six he towered over her own five foot four frame, his expensively tailored suit emphasizing his broad shoulders.

His wavy, blackish-brown hair was cut short and he wore a neatly clipped mustache and goatee that framed a mouth which somehow managed to look sensuous and cruel at the same time. But it was his eyes that really commanded attention. A pale ice-blue, fringed thickly with black lashes, they always managed to make Holly feel like her boss could see right through her clothes.

Yeah, right. Like he would want to. But still, she couldn't help fantasizing.

"Miss Sparks?" The frown on Mr. Harris's face let her know she'd waited too long to answer his question. "Daydreaming again?" he asked, one corner of his sensuous mouth quirking up.

"Oh, uh, no. No, of course not, Mr. Harris. And you look very nice. Very..." Holly reached for an appropriate word. *Hot. Tasty. Lickable.* "Professional," she said, giving him what she hoped was a business-like smile.

"Excellent. Just the look I was going for," he said dryly. "So, if you'll just hand me the briefing file I'll be on my way."

"Of course. I have it right..." Holly's words trailed off as her reaching fingers encountered empty air. Where was the briefing file? A knot of panic twisted her stomach. This was a very important board meeting and it was vital that Mr. Harris had everything he needed at his fingertips. But though she could have sworn the file was just there a moment ago, now it was gone.

"Miss Sparks? The file?" Mr. Harris was frowning now, his handsome face like a thundercloud.

"I...I...it was just here." Holly could feel her cheeks getting hot. Honestly this kind of thing never happened to her. She was usually so organized, so perfectly in sync with her boss's needs that he joked she would hand him a glass of water before he even knew he was thirsty. What had happened to that file?

"So you *lost* the file. Is that what you're telling me?" Mr. Harris took a step toward her, looming over her menacingly.

"I suppose so," Holly faltered. "But if you'll just give me a minute to look for it—"

"Oh, I'll give you more than a minute. If we're going to delay the board meeting it has to be for a good reason." Harris's deep voice was dangerously soft.

"Please..." Holly gasped but he was already calling the receptionist outside the board room on a holo-link. "Terri? Please inform the board members that we're going to be a little delayed getting started today. I have some *business* to attend to in my office that can't wait."

"Yes, Mr. Harris." The blonde head of the receptionist nodded and then popped out of existence as Harris canceled the link. Then he turned back to Holly. "I think, my dear, that it's time for a little discipline."

"Oh God, please..." Holly started backing away from him, her breath hitching in her throat. But despite the fear zinging through her veins there was another, stronger emotion filling her. Desire. It made her nipples into hard little points and her pussy was suddenly hot and wet and ready. Her eyes kept straying to her boss's large, well-shaped hands. To feel his big hand connecting solidly with her tender bottom, to writhe and squirm in his lap as he held her down and punished her...even though she knew it was wrong...the very idea pushed all her buttons.

And Grant Harris knew it.

"Stop right there." His tone was commanding and Holly froze in place, her sensible heels planted in the plush nap of the luxurious carpet that covered his office floor.

"Mr. Harris?" Her voice was high and uncertain and her heart was pounding like it was trying to get out of her chest.

Harris gave her a cruel smile. "Very good, Holly. I see you can still take direction." He walked to the huge oak desk and patted the edge. "Now come here and lean over my desk. It's time for your punishment."

Biting her lower lip, Holly sidled toward the desk. But before she could lean over it as he had ordered, Harris bent down and murmured in her ear, "First lift your skirt."

The heat between her legs went super nova and she was so wet she was afraid he would be able to tell if she raised her sensible black skirt. All she had on under it were a pair of little white panties and by now they would be almost see-through from her juices. What would she do if her boss found out how much his punishments turned her on?

"Raise your skirt," he said again, the menace back in his deep voice. "I'm warning you, Holly, either you raise your skirt and take your punishment like a good girl or I'll raise it for you. And if I have to do it, you won't be able to sit down for a *month*."

Moaning softly, Holly bent over the desk and hitched her skirt up to her thighs.

"Higher," Harris demanded. "You know what I want, Holly. Bare your ass for me *now* or face the consequences."

Knowing better than to disobey him, Holly raised the skirt up over her hips and leaned over the wooden desk.

"Very nice," her boss growled, reaching out to caress her shivering bottom with one large hand. "But I thought I told you to bare your ass. Take your panties off, Holly."

"Please, no," she pleaded frantically. If she took off her panties and he saw her pussy he would know beyond the shadow of a doubt how hot and bothered this little scenario was making her. Her cunt lips felt hot and swollen and her juices were already wetting the insides of her thighs. Holly was sure she would die of embarrassment if he saw her slick, hot pussy...if he knew how much she wanted him, how much she craved his punishment.

But Harris was relentless. "I *said* take off your panties, Holly," he commanded in that soft, dangerous voice that made her so hot and wet. "Take off your panties and spread your legs. If you don't I'll be forced to—"

"Playing X-rated fantasies about your boss again?"

Holly nearly jumped out of her skin as the voice of Abby, her best friend and roommate, penetrated the fog of lust that had clouded her brain and popped her fantasy like a soap bubble. Damn it, why did Abby have to interrupt right as she was getting to the good part? The fantasy was so vivid Holly had almost been able to *feel* the heat of her boss's hand on her ass and the cool wood of the desk under her fingertips. But the illusion was shattered now. Ripping the dream-viewer goggles off her face she turned to face her friend, trying to look innocent.

"Hey, you're home early." She shifted uneasily on the fake zebra skin couch she and Abby had bought together. Their living room was a mix of casual and funky—heavy on the funk, thanks to Abby. Holly hoped she wasn't blushing too much—with her fair complexion every time she was embarrassed it really showed.

Abby grinned. "Meaning you thought you had at least another hour to play out your twisted little fantasy before I interrupted you?" Sighing, she sank down on the couch beside Holly. "Honestly, don't you see enough of that man at work?"

"That's none of your business," Holly snapped. "And neither is what I have programmed on my dream-viewer. You're so nosey, Abby. I bet you'd read someone else's diary if they left it lying around too."

"Yup. If there were any juicy parts." Abby was completely unrepentant. "What I want to know is why you don't just go for it. I mean, you've been working for the guy for two years now and neither one of you is getting any younger."

"Thanks for reminding me." Holly sighed. There was no point in getting mad at Abby — they'd been best friends since their first year in college and she wasn't going to change now. "But there's no way I can just 'go for it,' as you put it, with Grant Harris."

"Why not?" Abby was chewing gum as always. She crossed her long legs and snapped a big pink bubble in Holly's direction. "You said he wasn't dating anyone else. And you know he's not gay."

"Why not?" Holly looked at her best friend in disbelief. Sometimes Abby could be so dense. "Several reasons, actually," she said, counting them off on her fingers. "Number one, he's my boss. I could and probably would get fired and then how would I pay my half of the rent? Number two, he's gorgeous and I'm...not."

Abby frowned. "Don't put yourself down, Holly, you're very pretty. I've always wished I could try my hair in your shade of red but there's no way I could pull it off without your peaches and cream complexion to go with it."

"It's not my hair and skin I'm worried about," Holly protested, putting a hand to her thick, curly auburn hair. "Although I *do* wish I didn't have freckles on my nose."

"The freckles are cute." Abby snapped her gum annoyingly. "With those big dark blue eyes of yours they make you look like the girl next door."

"A man like Grant Harris doesn't date 'the girl next door.' He's a freaking billionaire — he dates super models or whoever else he wants."

"No, he doesn't," Abby objected. "You told me you haven't seen him dating anyone since the first year you worked for him. As far as you can tell he's completely unattached — why shouldn't he give you a chance?"

"Because I'm not shaped like *you*." Holly eyed her best friend with resigned envy. Abby was built like a whippet, all long, lean limbs and perky teacup breasts topped off with luscious blonde hair. Not that whippets had perky breasts and blonde hair but still, the point was Abby was thin and Holly…was not.

"Don't start this again." Abby sighed. "You're thinner than you were in college, Holly and even back then you didn't look bad. It's all in your mind."

Holly stood up and pointed to her ass. "Does *this* look like it's all in my mind?"

Abby shrugged. "So you got a little junk in the trunk. So what?"

"So what? The point is no matter how much I diet and exercise, I'll still have these hips and this ass to deal with." Holly looked at her heart-shaped bottom sadly before sinking back down on the couch. She was a decent size up top with a nice C cup but from the moment puberty had struck at age twelve she'd had to deal with her oversized butt. The boys in high school had been merciless—some of the unkind names they called her still haunted Holly at night when she couldn't sleep.

"Your ass isn't that big—you're just still stuck in high school," Abby said, as though reading her mind. "And besides, some men like a little something to hold on to."

"Not men who own controlling interest in the largest hovercar corporation in the world," Holly said glumly. "Not men who can have their pick of any stick-thin skinny-minny they want."

"Hey, I resent that." Abby put a hand to her nonexistent hips. "I can't help being skinny. In fact, I wish I wasn't. I'd love to have your curves. I don't know why you never notice it but there are guys checking you out when we go out together—plenty of them."

"Yeah, right." Holly sighed. "Forget it, Abby, it's never gonna happen."

"Never say never." Abby grinned. "What if you somehow found out that Mr. Boss Man was into plus sized posteriors and didn't mind dating the help. Then what?"

"Um..." Holly could feel her cheeks heating again. "I still don't think it would happen." She didn't want to say why but it was clear that Abby had guessed the third and final reason she and her boss were never going to get together outside of a dream-viewer.

"You think he's not into that freaky shit you program into your viewer?" Abby smiled not unkindly. "That's it, isn't it?"

"I swear to God, Abby. Nothing is sacred with you, is it?" Holly frowned but her best friend just grinned and blew another juicy pink bubble.

"I'm right, aren't I?"

Holly sighed, defeated. "Yeah, you're right."

"Well that's crap," Abby announced. "You never know unless you try. If he's as big a control freak as you say, I bet he'd get off on all that dominance and submission stuff."

"Abby, please! That's completely out of the question." Holly felt like her whole body was blushing. There was no way she was going to approach her handsome, unobtainable boss and ask if he wanted to dominate her. In fact, the very idea of him finding out that she craved punishment from him was enough to make her feel slightly ill with embarrassment.

Abby grinned unrepentantly. "Suit yourself but I think you're passing up a golden opportunity. There must be some way you could let him know. Bring that dream-viewer to work and leave it on your desk come lunch time. If he's half as nosey as me he'll take a peek and before you know it he'll be calling you into his office and bending you over his knee."

"Don't even *talk* about that." Holly felt a flutter of pure panic at the very idea. If Grant Harris the Third ever, *ever* got even an inkling of the kind of sex she craved, let alone found out that she programmed her dream viewer with sick, naughty fantasies of him spanking her into submission she would absolutely *die*.

Abby looked bored. "Fine. We can discuss the juicy details of your real sex life instead. Oh wait—you don't *have* one because you're too in love with your boss to go out with the guys I set you up with."

Holly's hand tightened on the expensive dream-viewer headset. "It's not that I don't want to go—I just don't have time right now, Abby. I'm always away on business trips and I work nights and weekends half the time too."

"Only because you want to be near your precious boss," Abby accused. "Hell, if he decided to become a vampire and told you he was going to conduct business from midnight to dawn you wouldn't bat an eye. You can't even promise to spend Christmas with your family because he might want you to go somewhere."

Holly shifted uncomfortably. This had been a sore spot with her mom—leave it to Abby to bring it up. "It's just that Grant said we might go on a business trip around that time and I don't like to promise if I'm not sure I can keep my word."

"So now it's 'Grant' is it? Only I bet you never call him that at work. Anymore than he calls you Holly." Abby frowned.

"Well, no...but we have a formal relationship. There's a line we never really cross. Not that I don't want to but I *can't*." Holly felt frustrated, trying to explain. How could she make Abby see? Her friend was so blunt and straight-forward, there was no way she would get Mr. Harris's dry sense of humor. How could Holly explain the witty, acerbic little asides he murmured to her in the middle of boring business meetings when she was supposed to be taking notes for him? Or the way he looked at her sometimes with those piercing blue eyes as though he was trying to see her very soul?

Holly had seen the way other big finance and business men treated their personal assistants — like machines that were designed to do a specific task with no emotions or personal preferences. Mr. Harris wasn't like that. When they went out for lunch, he asked her where she wanted to go and always picked up the check. When they went on business trips he let her choose the hotel they stayed in. He took a personal interest in her, asking about her weekends and her family and listening intently to everything she said. They even traded favorite books back and forth on occasion.

And just because they retained their formal façade and called each other Mr. Harris and Miss Sparks didn't mean he didn't care — to Holly it meant that he respected her too much to treat her like an object or just another employee in his vast corporation. How could she help falling in love with him in light of those circumstances?

"Hello, Earth to Holly?"

"Huh?" Holly looked up to see Abby staring at her in disgust.

"Look, it's clear I'm getting nowhere with you. If you want to waste your life pining after a man you're too afraid to go after, then be my guest." Abby shook her head and stood up. "Just remember when you're old and gray and all alone it's because you were too chicken to take a chance."

"Thanks a lot," Holly muttered as her friend left the living room. For a moment she wondered if Abby might be right. She and Mr. Harris had a lot in common. Was it possible that her boss might share her sexual interests as well? And might he feel about her the way she felt about him?

Then sanity reasserted itself. No matter what a good, considerate boss Mr. Harris was, that was all he was—her boss. And he was so far above her he might as well be a star in the sky—something to wish on and dream about but not something she could actually ever have.

"Get over it, Holly," she told herself with a sigh as she grabbed the remote and flipped on the vid-wall. "You're his assistant, not his girlfriend. And that's how it's going to stay."

Chapter Two

Grant Harris the Third wasn't exactly sure when he'd fallen for his shy but intriguing assistant. Maybe it was the first time he'd heard her sexy little purr of a laugh. Or when he saw her reading a book that happened to be one of his favorites and found out it was her favorite too. Or maybe it was the first time he'd seen her bend over to pick something up and got to really appreciate that round, luscious ass she hid behind her boxy business skirts. Hell—maybe it was a combination of all those things. Whatever the cause the effect was the same—Grant wanted Holly like he'd never wanted a woman before.

Too bad she was off limits.

He paced around his spacious office, dictating business correspondence and watching her from the corner of his eye as she took notes on the iThink holo pad. The device was top of the line. It would record not just his image and words but his body temperature, heart rate and the mood he'd been in when the recording was made as well as Miss Sparks' private notes and reminders. And Grant was watching his assistant every bit as attentively as the machine was watching him.

Holly wasn't the kind of woman the world expected him to date—that was for sure. She wasn't super slim or tall or blonde and tanned. Her hair wasn't sleek and perfectly coifed. Oh, she always looked businesslike, twisting her auburn curls into a plump bun at the nape of her neck. But somehow a tendril or two always managed to escape their prison, giving her a sexy fly-away look. Instead of little black dresses she wore sensible heels and frumpy business clothes that didn't show her true shape although it was plain enough that she was full figured, especially around her ripe, squeezable ass. In fact, if Grant had been a different kind of man he would have had his hands on that ass a long time ago.

No, can't think like that, he reminded himself firmly as he went on dictating business by rote. *Holly's off limits and you know it.*

Grant knew he should just forget his assistant and try to start dating again which he hadn't been doing for the past year and a half since he realized Holly was the one he wanted. He ought to leave her alone and try to meet the kind of woman a man of his wealth and stature was supposed to go out with. The trouble was, he'd tried dating those women and they left him cold.

Running the largest hovercar corporation in the world didn't leave him a lot of time to meet people. So for a while he'd employed a dating service that catered specifically to the super rich. But all the girls they set him up with seemed to be the same—tall, skinny, and just a little too interested in his money. Grant would never forget the last "date" he'd gone on with one of these supermodel-type gold diggers.

The woman had been perfectly coifed, her platinum blonde hair piled into a gleaming mass on top of her head. She was bone-thin, her tan skin stretched tightly across her exotically high cheekbones—so tightly it looked like her skeleton was trying to get out of her body. Adding the hair-do to the five inch spiked heels she had strapped to her exquisitely pedicured feet, she was almost as tall as Grant.

On top of being a perfect ten, his prospective date had a pedigree as long as his arm—something that would surely please his family—not that Grant really cared. Being a debutant and having a blood line you could trace back to Plymouth Rock didn't automatically make a woman sexy or interesting or fun to be with. But the dating service had sent her so he felt it was his duty to at least *try*. Holly had only been working for him for about six months at that time and he hadn't yet realized his feelings for her so he'd had his date meet him at the office.

As he showed the tall blonde around, Grant had made a joke—he couldn't even remember what it was now—he was just trying to lighten the mood and get the date off to a good start. He would never forget the blank look on the stick-thin girl's face. He wasn't sure if she didn't think the joke was funny or if it had gone totally over her head. But as they'd left his office, he'd heard Holly's quiet, sexy little laugh. He'd turned back and raised an eyebrow at his assistant and she'd shrugged apologetically. "Sorry, I know that wasn't meant for me, Mr. Harris. It just tickled my funny bone."

At that moment it was as though he saw Holly—really *saw* her—for the first time. The date with the blonde debutant had tanked, of course but after that day he'd begun to pay more attention to his assistant. He asked about her life and started getting her opinion on certain decisions. What he learned astounded him. Holly had great business sense and a wonderful sense of humor. A sharp intelligence was hidden behind those innocent deep blue eyes and as he came to know her better, he realized that they had more in common than any of the women the dating agency sent over. Accordingly, he stopped his contract with them and just concentrated on getting to know his assistant. And over the last year and a half he had fallen for her completely.

So why wasn't he with Holly right now? Why didn't he have her sitting in his lap with her arms around his neck while he kissed her senseless instead of droning on and on about some boring business meeting he could conduct in his sleep?

It wasn't because she was his assistant. There were ways to work around that and he didn't give a damn what anyone thought even though he knew his father, Grant Harris the Second, would probably have an aneurysm if he knew Grant was dating "the help." Holly came from a middle class background with a mixed heritage that would make his mother cringe. But again, Grant didn't care.

And it wasn't because Holly wasn't the trophy wife he was expected to fall for. It didn't matter to him that she wasn't tall and thin. He was tired of taking tanned skeletons to bed. The last girl he'd slept with had been as flat as a boy with non-existent hips and an ass so tiny and tight you'd need a microscope to find it under her perfectly distressed three thousand dollar jeans. During sex their hip bones had knocked together painfully and there was nothing for Grant to hold onto. It was miserable.

In contrast, he could just imagine what sex with Holly would be like. Under those boring business skirt and jacket combos she always wore he could tell her body was ripe and firm. He wanted to hold her heavy breasts in his hands and thumb her nipples while she moaned his name. Wanted to part those lush thighs and lap her sweet cunt until she came for him again and again.

But he couldn't.

Because Grant needed more than intelligence and a good sense of humor in the woman he picked to stand by him for life. He needed more than shared interests, a pretty face, and a luscious body.

Grant needed a submissive.

A woman who was willing and eager to submit to him sexually, who wanted to be dominated in the bedroom. And someone who needed to be tied up, teased, and punished as much as Grant needed to hand out that punishment, was hard to come by.

If Holly had any idea of the hot, twisted things he wanted to do to her sweet little body, Grant was sure she'd run screaming for the nearest unemployment line. He hadn't spent the past year and a half falling in love with her just to lose her because of his deviant desires.

So Grant kept his mouth shut and his hands to himself. Better to have her in his life as an assistant and a friend than to not have her at all. Occasionally it got to be too much for him though, and he wondered if there was any way to find out if Holly might be open to his sexual needs. He'd had her followed by a private eye for a while but with disappointing results. Holly didn't frequent any of the D&S or S&M clubs in the city. In fact, she didn't go out much at all. She spent most of the time she wasn't at work in the small, eclectically decorated apartment she shared with her best friend, an irritating woman called Abby.

For a while Grant had even wondered if his assistant might be a closeted lesbian but the private eye nixed that idea, much to his relief. Holly never seemed attracted to other women and besides there was something—a spark of attraction between her and himself—that Grant was sure wouldn't have been there if she didn't have an interest in men. But as far as he had been able to find out, she lived the life of a nun—which made it even more likely that she'd run as fast and as far as she could get from him if he revealed what he fantasized about every time he saw her.

Pulling the clip out of her hair and putting her over my knee so that all those long red curls hang down as I push up her skirt. She'll struggle and cry while I pulled down her panties but we both know she needs to take her punishment. With the panties out of the way I can finally see the creamy, white skin of her luscious ass. Once I start spanking her all that beautiful pale skin will turn as red as a sunset and Holly will writhe and moan, begging me not to stop. To never stop...

"Mr. Harris—you were saying?"

He looked up to see Holly staring at him curiously, her fingers poised over the iThink. Great, apparently he'd drifted off to fantasyland in the middle of business dictation.

"I...um..." Grant cleared his throat, hoping his erection didn't show under his four thousand dollar suit pants.

This was ridiculous and incredibly frustrating. Grant had been born to wealth and privilege and for the past five years, since his father had passed the reins, he'd been running a multi-billion dollar company. He was a man who was used to having what he wanted and right now what he wanted was the girl sitting not ten feet away from him, waiting patiently for him to find his train of thought and continue dictating. The girl he could never have because he was afraid to scare her off.

Off limits, he reminded himself and cleared his throat. "I was saying that I, uh, I'm sorry, Miss Sparks but I'm afraid I'll have to take a business trip over the Christmas holiday after all. I'll understand if you can't come—I know you have family obligations this time of year and—"

"I'll come," she interrupted quietly. "Is it really being held on the moon?"

"Yes, it is. That's neutral ground for Psi-no Industries so it's the only place they'll agree to meet. Especially since they think we're trying to take them over."

"And are we? I mean, are *you?*" Holly corrected herself, blushing.

"Well, they *are* our biggest competitors and rumor has it that Howard Meeks, their CEO, is having some serious financial difficulties. I might consider it but it's a very delicate situation. You just can't force these things—it takes finesse." Grant squeezed one hand into a fist to illustrate his point. "Sometimes you have to dominate quietly by sheer force of will."

"Oh…oh really? You have to, uh, *dominate* them?" Holly's voice sounded slightly breathy. Grant wondered if he was imagining it—wishful thinking maybe?

"Yes," he asserted. "And once I determine if they're worth acquiring I'll make my move. Of course, the employees will be frightened at first. They'll think I want to do them harm—strip them bare and leave them naked and helpless."

"Naked and…and completely helpless," Holly repeated. Her cheeks were flushed and she was definitely breathing harder now. This time Grant was sure he wasn't imagining things.

"Yes," he murmured, taking a step toward her. "Of course, nothing could be further from the truth, Miss Sparks. The world perceives me as ruthless but I would never hurt anyone under me. I might have to *whip* them into shape a little and let them know I expect to be obeyed but I would never do them permanent or lasting harm."

"No...no of course you wouldn't." Holly was nearly panting now. "And if you had to whip them — punish them — it would only be for their own good."

Grant was intrigued. Was she actually getting turned on by his analogy? "You find the idea of a whipping intriguing, Miss Sparks?" he asked, watching her intently.

"Oh yes! I mean..." Holly looked flustered. "I mean, only if they *need* it. Those other employees, I mean."

"Of course," Grant murmured, smiling. "Only if they need it."

"So, accommodations." Holly cleared her throat and sat up straighter, obviously trying to get back to business. "Where would you like to stay during this trip?"

"You pick." Grant was sorry to leave their current topic of conversation but at least now he had food for thought. Maybe there was more to the demure Miss Sparks than met the eye? He certainly hoped so.

"The Pleasure Dome," Holly said, surprising him yet again with her choice of hotel.

Grant raised an eyebrow at her. "The Pleasure Dome? You *do* realize that's right in the heart of the red light district?"

"Yes, I realize that." She met his eyes with an obvious effort.

Grant shook his head. "I would have thought you'd choose the Moon Hilton or someplace equally prestigious and shall we say, less disreputable. Everyone knows The Pleasure Dome caters exclusively to tourists looking for sex, scandal, and general debauchery. Explain your choice."

Holly sat up straighter. "Staying at a hotel in the red light district instead of a more respectable location will throw Meeks off. He'll think you're there for the...distractions offered only on the moon instead of serious business."

Grant nodded thoughtfully. Holly was always full of surprises but this one was more surprising than most. Still, she had an excellent reason for her choice and he liked her logic. "A very good point," he said at last. "Very well, The Pleasure Dome it is."

"Excellent." Holly's slim fingers hovered over the iThink. "When do we leave and what's the length of our stay?"

"Hmm, it's a nine hour trip by private shuttle and then Meeks wants to meet on Christmas day—I think he thought stipulating that would make me back down. But since I'm not all that eager to eat my mother's latest efforts at roast goose, I agreed."

Holly made a face. "She's really going to cook a *goose?*"

Grant shrugged. "Her book club has been reading the classics lately and right now they're doing Dickens. If Christmas goose is good enough for Ebenezer Scrooge it's good enough for my mother."

She giggled and then tried to pull a straight face. "I'm sorry. That isn't funny."

"Actually, it is," Grant said mildly. "And it doesn't make it any easier that she never goes near the kitchen until this time of the year. She barely knows how to turn on the stove but she suddenly expects to be able to whip up a ten course holiday dinner—this year including a chestnut and sage stuffed goose with leek butter and lobster infused crème fresh."

"Ugh." Holly made a face. "Sorry but that doesn't sound very good."

"I don't expect it to be." Grant smiled at her. "Which is why I plan to be two hundred and thirty eight thousand miles away when it's served. And as there are bound to be many, *many* leftovers, I'm in no hurry to come back, either."

"I don't have any holiday plans either," Holly said, her fingers still hovering over the iThink.

"So then—shall we say we'll stay five days to a week? A little time for pleasure as well as business. You've never been to the moon, have you?" Grant asked.

She smiled slightly. "A ticket to the moon cost roughly what I make in a year. So, no, I've never been."

Grant frowned. "Hmm, we'll have to remedy that. I'll get in touch with human resources immediately and put you in for a raise."

"No, no. I mean—I wasn't asking for a raise." Holly's cheeks flushed with embarrassment. "I just meant that, uh, ordinary people like me don't usually get to go to the moon. That's all."

He leveled a look at her, holding her dark blue eyes with his gaze. "Miss Sparks," he growled softly. "I have known you for nearly two years now and I am convinced you are *anything* but ordinary."

"Oh...thank you." Holly looked flustered which pleased him immensely. Even though he couldn't have her, he still enjoyed making her blush.

"Book us into The Pleasure Dome for a week," he said, nodding at the iThink. "And be sure to get us the best rooms they have. We *non*-ordinary people have to travel in style." Already he was anticipating showing Holly everything the moon had to offer. The finest restaurants, the most cutting edge entertainment — he was going to take her everywhere.

This was going to be one business trip he really enjoyed.

Chapter Three

Holly couldn't believe her luck as she unpacked her suitcase in the lurid red and purple room at The Pleasure Dome. The moon—she was actually on the moon! Ever since she could remember it had been the ultimate dream vacation. Of course, when the lunar atmosphere domes had gone up around 2060, the government had been hoping to make it a new colony to ease the overcrowding on Earth. But the incredible cost of getting there and back again made it impossible for any but the very rich to make the trip. Accordingly, the moon had become the new Vegas, complete with ultra luxury hotels, high stakes gambling, and of course, sexual variety that couldn't be found anywhere else.

And it was this last feature that made Holly so glad she was finally here. Not that she was looking to hire a male escort—not exactly, anyway. But the moon was the home base of a company she'd done a lot of research on—Anyone U Want Androids Inc. In fact, from the moment her boss had told her they were probably going to take a business trip to the moon, it had been all she could think about.

Anyone U Want specialized in making very special and specific fantasies come true. If you wanted to do something to someone that you couldn't get away with in real life, Anyone U Want was the place to go. Want to sleep with your best friend's wife? Or kill your boss? Or spend time with a loved one who had passed on? Anyone U Want could arrange all of these scenarios and more with their specialized, customizable androids.

All you had to do was give them a recording of the person you wanted reproduced, a basic script of how you wanted the scene to play out, and twenty-four hours notice and you could have your fantasy down to the tiniest detail — at least that was what their brochure claimed. And Holly was desperate to believe it.

She would rather have died than admit it but the reason she'd chosen The Pleasure Dome over the Moon Hilton wasn't just what she'd told Mr. Harris about putting his competition off guard. It was also because The Pleasure Dome was only a few blocks from Anyone U Want. With any luck she'd be able to nip down and place her order tonight and then have her fantasy later on in the week. She could tell her boss that she was doing a little sightseeing and he would never suspect a thing — she hoped.

She could still remember the odd look he'd given her when she got all hot and bothered over his speech about dominating and punishing the new employees under his command if he chose to take over Psi-no Industries. Probably he thought she was a little crazy, but at least he'd been nice enough not to mention it again. Holly didn't know what had come over her but the way he'd been talking in that deep voice of his had just about pushed her over the edge. God, she needed this release so badly! She just hoped that the Anyone U Want fantasy would live up to her expectations.

It was going to be horrendously expensive, of course. The Anyone U Want fee was going to use up her entire Christmas bonus and then some. She'd be living on nutrient paste for a month just to make ends meet when this was over. But it was worth it — so totally worth it to have Mr. Harris the way she wanted him, the way she craved him so badly.

Holly's legs trembled at the very thought and she could feel her pussy getting hot and wet under the innocent cotton panel of her panties. God, to have him master her, dominate and punish her the way she needed to be dominated and punished! Even if it was only once in her life, she was sure she could live on the memories forever. And she would have to because she was fairly sure this opportunity was never going to come around again.

Digging through her suitcase for the tiny image-bee she'd packed with her favorite fantasy from her dream-viewer headset, she was surprised to find the headset itself among her things, along with the Anyone U Want brochure. She didn't remember packing it and in fact, she *never* brought it along on business trips. It was far too risky. Not that Mr. Harris would ever go through her things but still... Shaking her head she covered the offending piece of equipment with a bra and panty set made of pale green silk. She liked pretty underwear and this was the set she'd brought to wear during her Anyone U Want fantasy. Hopefully Mr. Harris — or the android representing him anyway — would be ripping it off of her sometime later this week.

The chronometer on her wrist beeped, reminding her that she only had an hour before her boss came back from his preliminary meeting. Meeks had insisted on seeing him alone so Mr. Harris had reluctantly left Holly at the hotel. But she knew the minute he got back he'd want to go over everything that had been said and done so she had to hurry.

Leaving the suitcase on the bed she snatched her room key-chip and ran out the door. The sooner she got her fantasy with the android Mr. Harris set up, the sooner she could come back and spend time with the real Mr. Harris.

Chapter Four

"Miss Sparks? Are you in there?" Back early from his meeting, Grant tapped gently on the connecting door between his room and his assistant's. There was no answer but the door was ajar and his gentle motion pushed it open. Looking inside he saw the plush king size bed made up in a scarlet and purple spread that matched the gaudy flocked velvet wallpaper on the walls. The Pleasure Dome liked to make the most of its reputation as a high class red light hotel and its kitschy décor reflected that right down to the crimson shag carpeting and the gold plated bathroom fixtures.

"Miss Sparks? Holly?" he said again, to be sure she wasn't in the bathroom. But she wasn't. Had she gone sightseeing by herself? The idea of innocent little Holly off on a trip through the moon's notoriously dangerous red light district made him distinctly uneasy. Where had she gone? And was she all right?

Without noticing what he was doing, he stepped further into the room, looking for clues to her whereabouts. Her suitcase lay open on the bed and lying on the top row of neatly folded business wear was something that caught Grant's eye — a pale mint green bra and panty set. It was lacy and feminine and naughty and just the thought of Holly wearing it and nothing else was enough to have his cock throbbing in a second.

God, just the idea of her soft little pussy barely covered by those pale green lace panties...Unable to stop himself, Grant picked up the pair of silky lace panties and rubbed them gently against his cheek. He could just imagine doing the same thing while Holly had the panties on. He would press his face against her cleft, feeling the heat of her cunt through the whisper-thin material, knowing she was getting hotter and hotter for him. Then he would slide his fingers under the lacy border and trace her swollen pussy lips, feeling her moisture collect on his fingertips as she moaned and he thrust deeper into her wet depths...

What's that? His eye landed on an expensive looking piece of hardware—a head set that fit over the eyes and ears with a tiny bud microphone that curved along the wearer's jaw. It was a dream-viewer, Grant realized as he dropped the panties back in the suitcase and picked it up. And an expensive one at that. This must be what Holly had used her last Christmas bonus on. But what was she watching on it?

Knowing he shouldn't do it, but helpless to resist this rare glimpse into his assistant's private life, Grant slipped the headset on and was immediately transported...back to his office.

"Miss Sparks, come here at once. I want a word with you," he saw himself saying. Only this image didn't look exactly like him — or at least he hoped not. The look on his face was stern, almost menacing and the tone of his voice was angry and impatient.

"Certainly, Mr. Harris. At once." Holly came into view wearing something he'd never seen her in. Was that a slave outfit? It certainly looked like one. She had on a tight black leather mini skirt that showed off her curvaceous ass and black thigh-high stockings that made him drool. Up top she had on a black leather corset type bustier that pushed her full breasts up and out, baring their tops and showing the faintest hint of pink areola. God, if she really did dress this way at the office, there was no way he would be able to keep his hands off her!

"That's far enough, Miss Sparks. Why are you walking? You know how you're supposed to approach me," dream Harris barked. Immediately dream Holly stopped in her tracks.

Grant continued to watch, his cock throbbing in his pants, as his assistant dropped to her knees and crawled as sinuously as a cat over to dream Harris. The short black leather skirt rode up her thighs as she moved, showing flashes of white lacy panties beneath. When she reached dream Harris's feet, she pressed herself against his legs submissively and murmured, "Yes, Mr. Harris. Have I done something wrong? Do you need to punish me?"

"I most certainly do." Dream Harris snapped his fingers at her. "That last letter you typed out for me was full of mistakes. Do you know what happens when you make mistakes, Miss Sparks?"

"I get a spanking?" Holly looked up hopefully, her full ass and hips twitching as she spoke what appeared to be the magic word.

Grant gasped aloud as he watched the fantasy play out, his hands clenching into fists at his sides. A spanking? Punishment? Could it be that Holly craved these things the way he craved to do them to her? He was hoping to see her get put over dream Harris's knee and spanked next but he was disappointed.

"Normally, yes, you do get a spanking," dream Harris was saying. "But I'm in a hurry today. This time I think we can dispense with the spanking and go straight to the next punishment. So..." He lifted Holly's chin and looked down into her wide, innocent blue eyes. "Suck my cock, Holly. Suck me hard and long until I come down your throat."

"Yes, Mr. Harris," she murmured breathlessly.

Grant watched in disbelief as she reached up and unzipped dream Harris's pants — pants that were, incidentally, identical to the ones he was currently wearing. Then she got out his cock which also looked uncannily like the real thing and began to suck him.

Watching her sweet pink lips close around the head of dream Harris's cock was almost too much for Grant. His shaft felt like it was made of lead, heavy and throbbing for release. Did Holly really want to do this? Obviously she must — why else would she concoct such an elaborate fantasy about it? God, were all her fantasies like this or had he happened to find the one anomaly in the bunch?

Flicking to the main menu, Grant glanced down the list of "dreams" on the viewer. Only to find that he was the star player in every single one of them. There were fantasies of him spanking Holly, trying her up, and punishing her in every way imaginable.

Grant was shocked. And here he'd thought she was so innocent! And in fact, she was — on the *outside*. She never actually did any of this — he knew from the months he'd had her followed by the Private Eye. It was her fantasy life that was extreme. He couldn't believe some of the things she wanted him to do to her. Just watching little clips of each "dream" was almost enough to make him come in his pants.

"Hello? Anyone there?"

The voice outside Holly's door accompanied by a soft knocking shocked Grant back to reality. Was it Holly back from wherever she had gone? If she caught him looking in her dream-viewer…

He had the head set off and was stuffing it back into the suitcase under the green bra and panties when the door opened and an unfamiliar face peered into Holly's room.

"Room service?" the girl asked hesitantly, no doubt seeing the wild look on Grant's face. "Is now a good time?"

"No," Grant snapped. "Come back later. *Much* later."

"Yes, sir." The maid bobbed her head and shut the door quickly, obviously glad to get away from him.

Grant breathed a sigh of relief. *That was close. Too close. Better leave everything like you found it and go back to your room.* But though he knew it was the right thing to do, he couldn't help lingering, wishing for just one more look at the dream-viewer. The sight of himself and Holly doing things he had fantasized about doing with her for so long was addictive. Knowing that he shouldn't, he reached into the suitcase one more time.

But instead of finding the head set of the dream-viewer again, his seeking fingertips brushed against something smooth and flat. Pulling it out he saw it was some kind of brochure. He was about to put it back and reach for the head set again when words printed in bright yellow type caught his eye.

Anyone U Want Androids Inc. can make your fantasy a reality! blared the screaming yellow letters. *Simply bring a recording of the person or persons you want reproduced and we can have your dream date ready in twenty-four hours.*

Dream-viewer forgotten, Grant sank down on the vivid purple and scarlet bedspread and poured over the brochure. Could it be that *this* was where Holly had gone? Had she decided to make the fantasies she'd put in her dream-viewer a reality? Was she even now down at the headquarters of this place, this Anyone U Want, placing an order for an android that looked…like *him?*

The thought blew his mind. But no — it couldn't be true — could it?

Only one way to know for sure!

Glancing at the address on the brochure once more time, Grant headed out the door. He had to see if Holly was really doing what he thought she was doing.

The moon's red light district was garish at night. Blinking neon holo-signs vied for his attention, their glare lighting up the atmosphere dome high above. There were sex bots on every corner and crowds of men wandering from brothel to brothel, each with different "specialties" to offer. The air was hazy with smoke and the scent of sex and alcohol drifted from every open doorway.

The more he saw of it, the less Grant liked the idea of Holly being out here on her own. He knew she probably didn't realize it but she was much too pretty to be wandering around down here after dark. He had just about decided that he would have to confront her and take her back to the hotel in the interest of her own safety, when he reached the door of Anyone U Want Inc.

He was about to go inside and look for Holly when he saw his curvy little assistant exiting the long, low building, her auburn hair glowing in the neon light. Standing in the shadows as he was, he could tell she couldn't see him. Should he go get her at once? Or just follow her from a safe distance to make sure she reached the hotel with no problems? He hated to embarrass her and he was certain she would be mortified if he caught her coming out of the android place— especially if she really was ordering what he thought she was.

Grant was still debating when he saw Holly hail a hovercab. It whizzed to the corner and picked her up, then hummed silently away.

He breathed a sigh of relief. Well, that was one problem solved — she would be safe in the cab. Now he could do what he had come to do and check on her order. Pushing through the sliding plasti-glass doors, he went inside.

"Hello, welcome to Anyone U Want. How can I help fulfill your fantasy?" a bored looking girl behind the front desk asked him.

"Well, it's not *my* fantasy per se that I'm here about."

She frowned. "I'm sorry, sir, but we have a strict confidentiality policy. I can't possibly let you view the details of anyone else's fantasy."

"Are you sure about that? Couldn't you just...*bend* the rules a little?" Grant gave her his most charming smile and made a five hundred credit marker appear in one hand.

The girl's eyes widened. Labor on the moon was cheap — this was probably more money than she saw in a month.

"Well..." She licked her lips nervously and glanced from side to side, as though making sure no one was watching. "I *guess* I could make one *tiny* exception."

Grant drummed his fingers impatiently as she pulled up the file.

"Here you go," she said at last, handing him her headset. "It's already uploaded to the main database and they're working on the android."

Grant watched the fantasy play out on her light screen and felt his trousers getting tight again. He had to shift from foot to foot, trying to make more room for his cock as he saw the naughty things Holly had planned. As he had thought, the android she was paying to play with was going to look like him...and it would be programmed to act as a Dominate to her sweet submissive.

Never in a million years would Grant have dreamed that his mild-mannered, sweet-natured personal assistant had such dark desires locked behind her innocent blue eyes. And to have the nerve to make her dreams a reality—well, in a manner of speaking anyway—it was more than he'd had the guts to do. All this time he'd been telling himself she was off limits, that he had to leave her alone so he wouldn't corrupt her with his deviant desires or scare her off completely and now...

Now I know she wants what I want, Grant thought suddenly. *She wants to submit and be dominated.*

And she would be too—by that damn android.

The idea of anyone else dominating Holly—even a soulless android—didn't sit well with Grant at all. He felt a possessive growl rise in his throat at the very thought. Holly was *his*, damn it! No one but he ought to be dominating her, pleasuring her, possessing her…

And no one's going to!

Suddenly, he had another idea. If Holly wanted her kinkiest fantasies fulfilled, then she was by-God going to get them fulfilled.

Giving the headset back to the girl behind the counter he made another credit marker appear—this one for a thousand.

"Tell me something," he said in a low voice. "How much would you charge to bend the rules just a little bit farther?"

The girl's eyes got even wider.

"What do you want me to do?"

"You don't have to do a thing," Grant assured her. "I'll take care of everything. Absolutely *everything.*"

Chapter Five

Holly looked around surreptitiously before stepping through the sliding multicolored plasti-glass doors of Anyone U Want. She wanted to be sure no one she knew could see her. It was a ridiculous idea, of course. Everyone she knew was over two hundred thousand miles away on Earth. Still, she couldn't help being nervous. The services that Anyone U Want provided were still new enough to be a grey area — both morally and legally. There were some who said the life-like androids should be outlawed and many, many others who thought anyone who used one was sick and depraved.

So what if I'm sick and depraved, Holly told herself, getting fed up with the fear. *I'm also desperate — this is the only way I'll ever get to have Grant on my own terms. I might as well enjoy it.* Lifting her chin, she marched through the garish doors and into a scarcely less garish interior.

Inside, Anyone U Want, had been made up like an old fashioned bordello. There was red velvet and dim lighting everywhere, making it clear that while some people probably *did* pay to see an android that looked like their dear departed loved one, most of them just wanted to fuck.

Which was exactly what she was here to do, Holly reminded herself. And even though her boss had been called to a last minute ultra-private meeting, she still wasn't sure how long said meeting would last. Well, as long as it lasted at least an hour she should be okay—that was how long the fantasies lasted here at Anyone U Want. Holly just hoped they had her Grant android all primed and ready to go. She had the mint green panty and bra set on under her business clothes and she was so nervous and turned on she thought she might faint. If she had to wait or God forbid, come back another day, she just might *die*.

"Hello, can I help you?" A bored looking young woman asked from the front desk.

"Oh!" Holly realized that despite her earlier determination, she'd just been standing there in the middle of the Anyone U Want lobby, nibbling her lower lip. "Yes," she said, making herself approach the desk. "Yes, you can. I...I've come about my fantasy."

"And your name is?" The attendant snapped.

"Uh...Holly. Holly Sparks. I was here earlier? I dropped off all my specifications and paid already." Holly wanted to make that crystal clear. There was no way she could afford to pay the huge sum of money she'd put down for this fantasy again.

"Oh yes..." The young woman scrolled through her listings on the midair screen in front of her and then shot Holly a strange look. "Sparks, you say?"

"Yes. Is there something wrong?" The way the attendant was looking at her was giving Holly a nervous case of the butterflies.

"No—not a thing." For some reason the girl gave her a secretive smile. "Your fantasy is all ready, Holly. And I think you're really, *really* going to enjoy it." Then she actually *winked*.

Holly bit her lip, feeling a blush rise hotly to her cheeks. Was it really necessary for the girl to tease her about her naughty fantasy? It seemed really rude to make such a personal comment—especially when Holly had paid so much for a private encounter.

"Thank you," she said stiffly. "Um, where should I go?"

"We have the stage all set up for you—area twenty-five." The girl pointed down a long corridor behind her desk. "Don't worry—all areas are soundproofed so you can, ah, have as much *fun* as you like."

Holly's face was so hot now she felt like her hair was going to catch on fire.

"Fine," she said woodenly.

"Oh—and don't forget, your fantasy won't officially begin until you say the words 'Start Fantasy.' So even once your, uh, *android* enters the room, you can do whatever you want to him and he won't do anything back until you say that."

Holly knew all this already—she'd read about it in the brochure.

"All right."

"And if any time you feel uncomfortable, you only have to say, 'Stop Scene' and the, uh, *android* will stop."

Holly knew this too.

"Thanks. And I assume I have an hour, as specified on the contract?"

"Actually, you can have as much time as you want." The girl smiled sweetly. "Don't worry about it—it's all taken care of."

All taken care of? What the hell does that mean?

But Holly didn't want to ask. She just wanted to get away from the smirking attendant and get to her fantasy before she completely lost her nerve.

"All right," she said again and rushed past the rude desk attendant down the long corridor, her heels clattering nervously on the bare concrete floor. She counted off the doors as she went, noticing that some "areas" seemed to take more space than others. At last, when she finally got to the small door marked Area 25 in faintly glowing holo-letters, she let herself breathe.

She reached for the knob of the door...but her hand trembled and she hesitated. This was it—the moment she'd been waiting for and dreaming of for so long. The moment she'd paid so much money for she was going to be on a starvation diet for the next several months. The moment of no return.

If I do this, will I ever be able to look Grant in the eyes again? Holly asked herself. *Will I ever be able to take dictation or plan his schedule without remembering that I let an android that looked exactly like him do all the things I wish he would do to me?*

Then again, she would kick herself if she lost this opportunity. Especially since the money was already gone from her bank account.

Taking a deep breath, Holly twisted the knob and let herself in. An exact replica of her boss's office back home greeted her.

"Wow," she muttered, her heels sinking into the plush carpet as she stepped into the room. There was Mr. Harris's polished wooden desk with its high-backed padded chair and there was her own, smaller chair to one side of it. There was a window — no doubt a holographic reproduction but very good all the same — that showed the same remote view of the city she looked out at every day. There were even stacks of paperwork and an iThink holo pad lying on the desk waiting for her to work on it.

But where was the main attraction? Where was the android Grant Harris?

As if answering her thoughts, the knob turned and the door opened to reveal her boss.

"Hello, Ms. Sparks," he said curtly, exactly as he always did every morning. Then he went to sit behind his desk and started looking through the papers stacked there.

Holly couldn't help but gape at him in astonishment. She'd seen the ads for Anyone U Want often enough to have them memorized but none of them had ever shown an android that looked this *realistic*. Most of the androids she'd seen had slightly plastic looking skin and glassy eyes. Holly had been prepared to ignore these slight flaws — as long as the android looked like a reasonable facsimile of her boss and was able to do everything she wanted, it was good enough for her.

But this...this was *amazing*. She took a step closer to the android boss, still bent studiously over his paperwork. She wanted a closer look at the Grant android...and then she remembered she could actually *have* one.

The fantasy doesn't start until I say, she reminded herself. *Until then, I can do anything I want.*

Including getting close to her boss in ways she'd always dreamed of but never dared.

Holly knew she was safe but still, he looked so real it took a moment for her to gather her nerve. Only the knowledge that the clock was ticking got her moving. The real Mr. Harris would be certain to be suspicious if he came back from his meeting and found her gone.

She came around the desk as she did every day. But this time instead of sitting down in her chair and going over the day's schedule, Holly stepped boldly up to her boss. He was so much taller than her that they were almost an even height, even with her standing and him sitting.

The android Grant took no notice of her so Holly began to feel brave. She took a closer look—yes, it was Grant Harris the Third, all right—right down to the dimple on his left cheek and the small touches of silver in his dark hair, right at the temples. He really was a mouthwatering man.

Daring greatly, Holly did something she'd always wanted to do and ran a hand through his hair. For a moment, she almost thought she felt the android shudder, its big frame moving beneath her touch. But Grant continued to stare down at the paperwork and she concluded she must have been mistaken.

Getting braver, Holly lifted his chin, relishing the slight scratch of his whiskers against her palm, and looked into his eyes. They didn't look glassy or artificial at all. In fact, they were the exact same pale, icy-blue shade, fringed thickly with black lashes that she looked at every day.

"Amazing," Holly whispered to herself, stepping even closer, so that she was between the android's spread legs. "It's so *real*."

Still the Grant android said nothing. It only stared at her with an inscrutable gaze as Holly ran her fingers through its thick, dark hair as she had always longed to do with the real Grant. He even smelled real—the warm, spicy scent of his expensive cologne filled her senses, making her almost dizzy with desire.

Then she did something else she'd always wanted to do. Cupping his strong jaw in her hand, she bent down and kissed the sensuous mouth.

The android's lips were pliant under hers and for a moment—just a bare moment—Holly thought she felt him kissing her back. But when she pulled back uncertainly, he stopped at once. Feeling reassured, Holly went back to her kiss. Grant's mouth tasted of the spearmint candies he liked to suck between meetings—sweet and sharp and hot—so hot. How did they get an android to have such lifelike body temperature?

Somehow she found herself sinking into his lap with her lips still locked with his. God, he felt so solid—so muscular and firm beneath her, just like she'd always imagined the real Grant would. She knew he worked out on a regular basis and she'd seen his broad, muscular chest once or twice when he had to change quickly in the office—she wondered if the android did justice to that particular detail? And speaking of details...

"Oh!" she jumped, breaking the kiss as she felt something hot and hard pressing against her ass. Well, *that* was surprising. Could the Anyone U Want people really make androids that got hard-ons?

Standing up, she reached boldly into his lap to find out. The android Grant was wearing an expensive looking, dark, tailored suit exactly like the kind the real Grant always wore. Sure enough, tenting the crotch of the suit was a long, hard ridge that must be his cock.

Mesmerized, Holly reached down to touch it. Then she gripped it gently in her hand, marveling over the size. Wow — she hoped she'd be able to handle all this! She didn't know if it was true to life or not but it was clear that here at Anyone U Want, size mattered.

Again, as she stroked the hard ridge, she thought she felt the Grant android quiver. But his expression remained blank and Holly decided she must have imagined it. She stroked him again, feeling the heat of his thick shaft in her hand. Would she have that inside her soon? According to her fantasy she would. The very thought made her shiver.

At last, Holly stopped and stood back. Kissing and touching him was fun, but the clock was still running. And no matter what the girl at the front desk had said about everything being taken care of, she didn't want to get only halfway through and then be told her time was up and she had to leave.

Still, she couldn't help stealing one last kiss.

"Mmm," she murmured, pressing her lips to his mouth. "I've wanted to do all that for just about forever, I think. I don't care if I'll be living on nurtri-paste for a month—this is *totally* worth it."

Then she stepped back and went to sit at her own chair beside his desk. Clearing her throat, she raised her voice and said clearly, "Fantasy Start."

Chapter Six

When he heard her say, "Fantasy Start," Grant breathed a sigh of relief. God, now he could *finally* take some action—which was good. He'd thought he was going to go crazy when Holly had come up to him and started running her soft fingers over his jaw and through his hair. And then when she'd started kissing him and stroking his cock through his trousers, he'd been sure he was going to *explode*.

Who knew his shy, innocent assistant had so much sexual frustration pent up inside…or such a soft and sexy touch? And when she'd said she'd been wanting to kiss him and touch him forever…well, Grant felt exactly the same way. He'd almost admitted that he wasn't an android right then and there…but that would spoil her fantasy. He liked the way she was so uninhibited with him because she thought he wasn't real. He wanted that to continue. And besides, now he could give her what she'd been waiting for.

What they'd both been waiting for, for so damn long.

"Miss Sparks," he said, as he always did when they were working together and he wanted her attention.

"Yes, Mr. Harris?" Holly looked up demurely, her cheeks pink, her eyes bright with anticipation. God, he wanted her! But Grant knew he had to play this right.

"Do you have the Hastings file?" he asked, just as her pre-written fantasy script had specified. A large transfer of credit to the girl behind the front desk had allowed him a look at it, as well as the ability to switch with the android—which didn't look anything like him, in Grant's opinion.

"Oh, uh..." Holly scanned through her iThink quickly and then looked up at him. "I...I thought I had it but it's gone. I...I'm so sorry, sir."

Grant frowned. At this point he was supposed to take her over his knee and spank her, but he wanted to do something a little different. He wondered if she would be suspicious if he varied slightly from her fantasy. But the eager look in her eyes and the blush on her cheeks made him decide—he didn't want to just follow the script.

"Come here," he ordered, standing up so that he towered over her. From what he'd seen of her fantasies, Holly liked their height difference and he intended to make the most of it.

"Yes, sir." Holly came to him obediently and stood in front of him, her eyes downcast like a proper submissive.

"Very good. Now, Holly..."

Her eyes flashed as she looked up at his unaccustomed use of her first name but Grant went on.

"Holly," he said again. "Why do you always wear these boxy business clothes?"

"What?" She looked completely uncertain now. This clearly wasn't in her script. Still, Grant decided to go with it.

"I said, I don't like the clothes you're wearing," he said bluntly. "They hide your shape. And Holly…" He cupped her cheek and lifted her chin, looking into her eyes. "I like your shape. I *love* it."

"You…you do?" She was still looking at him uncertainly, nibbling that lush lower lip of hers.

Slowly, he nodded. "I do. So take off your clothes."

"What? But that's not part of the script. I—"

"Did you hear me?" Grant let his voice drop to a low, menacing growl as he held her eyes with his. "Take…off…your…clothes."

"I…I…" Holly's fingers dropped to her white business blouse and she began to fumble with the buttons.

Grant decided to take pity on her.

"Don't worry, Miss Sparks," he murmured, stroking her cheek gently. "I'll allow you to leave your underclothes on…for now, anyway."

"All...all right," she stuttered.

Somehow she managed to get her blouse unbuttoned, although her fingers seemed to be moving slowly and clumsily. Probably she was still in shock that her fantasy was turning into something she hadn't expected. But she wasn't backing out either and she hadn't said the magic words — "Stop Scene" — that would end her fantasy either. Grant had promised himself that no matter how much he wanted her, he would stop if she said them. They were her safe word in this scenario and, as a good Dom, he always honored safe words.

He waited patiently as the white blouse fluttered to the floor and she finally got her skirt unzipped and let it fall as well. His cock surged as he saw that she was wearing the mint green bra and panty set he'd seen in her suitcase. God, she looked luscious with her auburn hair tumbled around her shoulders and the tops of her breasts heaving as she tried to control her erratic breathing. Finally he could see all her lush curves — all on display just for him — and the sight was enough to make him ache for her.

Holly was trembling, fully into the fantasy now, her big eyes filled with fear. Part of him wanted to take her into his arms and soothe her — to stroke her and give her pleasure until she moaned and came for him. There was more to being a Dom than spankings and bondage, as he well knew. It was also important to emotionally dominate your sub—to let her know that she was no longer in charge of her own body—that she belonged to you completely. You didn't have to whip or bind her to get that message across.

But of course, Holly had come here looking for something very specific from him. And Grant was determined to give it to her. But not...quite...yet.

"You look lovely, Holly," he told her, his voice coming out slightly hoarse. God, that was an understatement! He could see the tight points of her rosy nipples pressing against the thin satin fabric of the green bra, and the soft little slit of her pussy was clearly outlined by her panties. He wondered if she was getting wet yet.

"Thank you, Sir," she whispered, looking down submissively.

"I've always wondered what you looked like without your clothes," Grant went on. He took a step closer, deliberately crowding her.

"You...you have?" She risked a quick glance up at him.

"Yes, I have." Grant brushed a curly sheaf of auburn hair away from her neck and leaned down to kiss her gently on the delicate column of her throat. This was a very sensitive area, he knew and he could feel her quiver as he ran his tongue gently down the side of her neck, tasting her sweet, salty skin.

Holly stiffened and let out a little gasp...but held her ground as he licked her.

Grant was determined to get more of a reaction out of her. Taking her by the shoulders, he turned her firmly so that her back was to his front. Then he pulled her against him, making sure she could feel the hard ridge of his cock digging into her softly rounded ass.

"Oh, God," Holly whispered as he cupped her breasts. "Oh...Oh Grant!"

Her use of his first name—the only time she'd ever dared to call him that—gave Grant a fierce desire to turn her around and kiss her senseless. But he knew he couldn't give in to his urges—not yet. First he wanted to give Holly her fantasy.

"That's Mr. Harris to you," he growled menacingly, using his best Dom voice. "Or Sir or Master if you're so inclined."

"Yes, Sir. I'm sorry, Sir," Holly apologized breathlessly.

"That's all right, Holly. I accept your apology." Slowly, Grant reached around her and cupped her full breasts in his hands. "Which is why I'm only going to give you a very mild punishment for daring to use my first name."

"P-punishment?" she stuttered and he felt her shiver in his arms.

Slowly he pulled down the cups of her bra, baring her full breasts and hard nipples for him. Holly moaned softly as he filled his hand with her creamy globes, his thumbs moving with lazy flicking motions over her tight, pink peaks.

"That's right, Holly. First you lost the file I needed and then you called me by my first name. I think that deserves a punishment—don't you?" he murmured as he teased her.

"Y-yes, Sir. I...I suppose I do. Oh!" she gasped as he took her nipples between his fingers and squeezed tightly.

"And what do you think that punishment should be?" Grant mused softly, speaking in a low voice in her ear. He could feel her lush form trembling against his own, much larger body, could hear the breathless need in her voice. God, he wanted to slip the crotch of her panties aside and take her right here and now. But he couldn't...he needed to take this slowly. And besides, he wanted to savor Holly's first surrender to him. Her first, because if he had his way, there would be many, many scenarios like this to play out in the months and years to come.

"I...I don't know what my p-punishment should be," Holly moaned as he tugged on her tight little peaks. God, her breasts were so lush and full! He could spend hours just teasing them but Grant needed to move on to other things.

"I'll show you then—shall I?"

With one arm, Grand swept the paperwork off the desk and felt a tingle of satisfaction. How long had he fantasized about doing this? Pushing everything to one side and focusing his complete attention on his lovely little assistant? And tonight that fantasy was coming true.

He positioned Holly so she was standing right in front of the broad, wooden desk and put a hand on the back of her neck.

"Bend over the desk," he growled softly in her ear. "Do it, Holly. And then spread your legs. Spread them as wide as you can. Do you understand?"

She whimpered softly so he repeated the question.

"I said—do you understand?"

"Y-yes," she whispered. "I...I understand. But what are you going to do to me?"

"I told you," Grant murmured in her ear. "I'm going to *punish* you."

With Holly bending over the desk, her hands and cheek pressed to its shiny surface, he was free to at last admire that full, heart-shaped ass that had been the star of so many of his own fantasies for the last few years. He loved her hips too—so soft and curvy, so perfect to hold on to. But first he wanted to get his hands on that ass.

Lightly, he ran a hand down her back, from the vulnerable nape of her neck all the way to the rounded tops of her buttocks.

Holly gasped and her hands clenched into fists but she didn't move. Good. Grant smiled to himself. Then he leaned over her again and breathed in her ear,

"I thought I told you to spread your legs."

"I…what?" She turned her head, looking at him as though she couldn't quite believe it.

"You heard me. Spread your legs, Holly." Grant made his words come out deep and stern again—not difficult since it was almost always the usual pitch of his voice. But tonight he was being even more deliberate with his wording and tone.

Holly moaned but seemed reluctant to follow orders.

"All right, then," Grant told her, taking a firm grip on her full hips. "I'll spread them for you."

With that, he kicked her ankles apart, forcing her to spread wide so that she was neatly displayed on the desk with her ass high in the air.

"Oh!" Holly gasped but made no move to try and stop him. She just lay there quivering and spread for him.

Grant felt a surge of possessiveness rush through him at the sight of her sweet submission. *Mine,* a voice growled in his head and he knew it was true. Holly belonged to him—he just had to claim her.

But he didn't want to rush things.

"Good girl," he murmured. "Such a good girl to spread your legs for me, sweetheart. Look at this lush ass of yours," Cupping the curve of her cheeks, he ran one hand all over the sleek, shiny, mint green satin that was stretched tight across her generous globes. "I've always wanted to get my hands on your sweet ass," he informed Holly, as he stroked her, letting his fingertips stray dangerously close to the soft cleft of her pussy.

"You...you have?" She glanced back over her shoulder, disbelief clear in her big eyes.

"Always," Grant assured her. "You wear those boxy skirts all day and the only time I really get a good look at it is when you drop something and have to bend over and pick it up. And every time I see it I just want to pull you over my knee."

"You do?" Holly looked back at him, her eyes wider and wider. Maybe he was straying too far from the script. He didn't want her to get so nervous she stopped the fantasy.

Grant decided to give her what she wanted.

"Yes," he growled. "I want to pull you over my knee and spank that lush bottom of yours to punish me for cock-teasing me, Holly. For making it so damn hard to concentrate on work because all I can think of is taking you." He stopped stroking her bottom abruptly and hooked his fingers into the waistband of her mint green panties. Then he yanked them down. "Which is why I'm going to spank you *right now*."

* * * * *

Holly moaned softly as the android Grant pulled down her panties, baring her ass completely. Oh God, it was finally happening—she was finally going to get a punishment from her stern and sexy boss! Who cared if he was just an android—this was what she'd been wanting for *years*. And now she was finally going to get it!

For a while there, she'd been uncertain about what was going on. The android had appeared to go off script, first making her strip down to her bra and panties and then saying all kinds of things Holly hadn't written. She'd almost stopped the fantasy several times because she thought something might be wrong. But the android Grant was making her feel incredible and doing all the right things—even if they weren't the things she'd specified. Holly had been too into the scene to stop it and now she was glad she hadn't—she was finally going to get her spanking.

She waited for the first blow to fall but her android boss didn't spank her—instead he leaned over her, pressing his cheek to hers, letting her feel the rough scratch of his business suit against her bare skin.

"Now Holly, shall we do a little experiment?" he breathed in her ear, making her squirm. "Shall we see how this spanking is going to affect you?"

"What?" Holly turned her eyes up to his. "What do you mean? How?"

"I mean I want to see how wet your pussy gets when I spank you." He straightened up and then reached one large hand between the edge of the desk and her abdomen. Holly sucked in a breath as she felt his fingers slip down to cup her between her legs.

"Oh!" she moaned as she felt her pussy settle into his large, warm hand. "Oh, please..." They were going off script again and she didn't know if she ought to stop the scene or not. But it felt so good — too good to stop. She moaned again as two long fingers parted her swollen outer pussy lips and slipped into her inner folds, bracketing her sensitive little clit.

"Miss Sparks, your pussy is already quite wet," Grant murmured, his voice convincingly hoarse as he spoke. "Is that from the attention I paid to your sweet breasts and nipples earlier or because you're anticipating your punishment?"

"I...I don't know," Holly stuttered. "I don't...what makes you think punishment makes me...makes me..."

"Wet?" he finished for her in a soft voice. "What makes me think that punishment makes your sweet little cunt all hot and creamy for me? Maybe the way you feel against my fingers." He rubbed gently, massaging her clit.

Holly moaned and writhed helplessly against his invading fingers. Oh God, that felt so *good.* It was too bad this wasn't the real Grant — although she knew she would die from humiliation if it was. Of course, there was no way her real boss would manhandle her body like he owned her or speak such filthy language as he touched her but the fantasy she and the android were playing out was *amazing* even if it wasn't real.

"Let's put it to a test, shall we?" Grant purred in her ear. "I'm going to keep my fingers right here, in your plump little pussy while I spank you with my other hand, Holly. Let's see if getting punished makes you wetter."

"I...I..." Holly didn't know what to say. She had never written anything like this in her script. She never would have even *thought* of anything like this. And yet, she had never been hotter in her entire life.

"I'm going to give you ten strokes," the Grant android continued. "Two for losing that file, two for using my first name, and the rest for making my cock so fucking hard for the past two years. Count with me, Holly."

Raising the hand he wasn't touching her with, he let the blow fall. *Smack!*

"One."

Holly jerked and gasped as the pleasurable pain zinged through her. The motion caused her clit to rub against the two fingers Grant had firmly buried in her pussy, sending sharp little sparks of sensation all through her. Oh God, had she ever been so hot in her life? Holly didn't think so. Here she was, spread over her boss's desk with her panties down to her ankles and his long fingers in her wet folds while he spanked her, just as she'd always wanted him to. This fantasy was absolutely worth every penny she'd paid for it.

"I said, *count with me.*"

The android Grant's deep voice — so exactly like her real boss's voice that Holly honestly couldn't tell the difference — cut off her train of thought abruptly.

"Y-yes, Sir," she whispered. "One."

"And two..." *Smack!* He spanked her again and Holly bit back a cry. God, it hurt and felt good at the same time! She could feel her pussy getting wetter and wetter and her pleasure building as the movement made his long fingers rub even harder against her throbbing clit.

Smack!

"Three..." Holly gasped, the breath hitching in her throat. "Four...five..."

The spanking went on and on. And even though her backside felt like it was on fire, Holly never wanted it to end. Finally she was submitting to her dominant boss the way she had always fantasized. Finally she was getting what she had always craved.

At last, however, they reached "Ten" and Grant stopped spanking her. Instead, he rubbed a soothing hand over her stinging bottom, murmuring appreciatively about how lovely she looked with her ass all red.

"Your soft little pussy seems to have benefited from your punishment too," he added, lightly caressing her clit with just his fingertips until Holly moaned. "In fact, let's turn you over and see exactly how much."

Before Holly could protest, he had flipped her over so that she was lying on her back on the desk and stripped her panties the rest of the way off.

"Mr. Harris!" she gasped.

"Relax, Holly," he murmured, spreading her legs. "I just need to see if your spanking made your pussy even wetter than it was."

Holly bit her lip uncertainly as her boss spread her pussy lips and slid two long, strong fingers deep into her inner depths.

"Oh!" she gasped as he reached bottom inside her.

"Mmmm..." Grant thrust gently into her, sliding his long fingers in and out of her tight, slippery well. "Feel that, sweetheart?" he murmured, his eyes half-lidded with lust. "Do you feel how wet and hot me spanking that soft bottom of yours made you?"

"I...I guess it did," Holly admitted breathlessly. "I guess maybe...maybe I needed to be punished. I..." She bit her lip. "I've been needing it for years, ever since I came to work for you."

"And have you ever let anyone else punish you?" the Grant android demanded. There was a possessive light shining in his eyes that Holly thought was masterful workmanship. How *did* the Anyone U Want people make their androids so *lifelike?*

"No," she whispered, which was the truth. "I've only…only ever wanted to let *you* punish me, Mr. Harris. Just you…no one else."

"Good girl," he growled softly, still stroking into her with his fingers. "I'm the only one who should punish you, who should touch and spank and dominate you. The only one who should make you come. That was absolutely the right answer, Holly. And for that, I am going to reward you."

"You are?" Holly stared at him, wide-eyed. This was also off script, but at this point, she didn't even care anymore.

"I am." Grant leaned down so that he was looking directly into her eyes. "And do you know what good girls get, Holly?"

"N-no," she whispered.

A slow, hungry smile spread over his sensuous mouth.

"Holly," he murmured. "Good girls get *special kisses.*" Then he withdrew the two fingers he'd been slowly pumping into her pussy and slipped them into his mouth instead.

Holly gave a little moan as she watched him lick her juices, sucking hungrily to get all of her sweet honey off his fingers.

"God," he muttered, his voice thick with desire. "You taste even better than I thought you would, sweetheart."

"I...you..." Holly didn't know what to say. Luckily, she didn't have to speak.

Grant grabbed the high-backed office chair and adjusted it, then pulled it up to the desk and sat down right between her legs.

"Spread your thighs wider for me, Holly," he commanded in a low, lustful voice. "I'm going to taste your sweet little pussy until you come for me."

Holly cried out as he bent his head and she felt his hot breath caressing her open folds. And then he was kissing her—kissing her softly at first, almost as though he was kissing her mouth. But the tender oral assault soon changed as kissing turned to lapping and lapping to swirling.

As his tongue became bolder and began sliding deep into her wet, swollen pussy, Holly began moaning steadily. Oh God, was this really happening? Was she really lying here on her stern boss's desk with his face buried between her legs and his tongue exploring her pussy?

She'd always dreamed about this act, but she'd been too shy to write it into her fantasy. Even in her wildest dreams, she hadn't been able to convince herself that Grant Harris the Third would want to go down on her. He was, after all, a billionaire—one of the most powerful executives in the world. Why would he lower himself to bring her pleasure with his mouth? And yet he—or rather the android representing him—seemed to relish the act.

She jumped and cried out as he sucked her swollen clit into his mouth and lashed it with his tongue. Oh God, if he didn't slow down she was going to come. She could feel the pleasure building inside her with every move of his talented tongue.

The android Grant seemed to know she was close. He looked up briefly and locked eyes with her.

"Come for me, Holly," he ordered, slipping his long finger back into her quivering pussy. "Come hard—all over my face. I want you to."

Then he leaned down again and began lashing her clit with his tongue while he fucked deeply into her with his fingers.

Unable to hold back anymore, Holly obeyed her boss. With a low gasp, she felt herself reaching the edge and being pushed over—as much by his masterful words as the way he was touching and tasting her.

"Grant...oh, *Grant*," she moaned, forgetting she wasn't supposed to call him by his first name. Somehow her fingers slid into his thick, dark hair and she found she was pulling him forward, urging him on as she bucked up to meet his tongue and her orgasm spilled over her in a warm flood.

Grant rode out her pleasure, eagerly lapping her pussy, catching every drop of her honey as she cried and gasped. Then, when the last tremor had left her body, he rose and leaned over her, pinning her to the desk.

"God, you're delicious," he murmured, his eyes half-lidded and hungry. Wrapping one hand in her hair, he pulled her close and took Holly's mouth in a searing kiss, feeding her the taste of herself on his tongue.

"*Mmm.*" Holly kissed him back, licking hungrily. Who knew her secret flavor could taste so good on his lips, in his mouth? She could feel his weight on her body and the hard ridge of his cock branding her inner thigh. She didn't care anymore that this was an android and not her real boss—she wanted him more than she had ever wanted anyone.

"Please, Grant," she whispered, when the kiss finally broke. "Please take me. I...I need you."

"I need you too, Holly." His deep voice was hoarse, the look in his eyes so real she was almost fooled into believing it was her actual boss who spoke for a moment. "I've needed you for a long time."

"Then take me." Holly took a deep breath. "*Fuck* me," she breathed. "Fill me up with yourself and own my body…you…you already own my heart."

She didn't know where such brazen words came from…or why she chose to speak her innermost secret feelings when she knew this wasn't real. But she couldn't help herself — the android seemed so lifelike — so realistic. It was hard not to let her emotions run away with her when she'd just had such a mind-blowing orgasm.

"Oh, Holly. My sweet little Holly," he murmured, nuzzling her neck and looking into her eyes. "I *am* going to fuck you, sweetheart. Fuck you long and hard and deep until I make you mine…until no other man in the whole damn universe will ever dare to come near you again."

With that, she heard the low purr of his zipper coming down and then the blunt head of his shaft was nudging her folds open.

Eagerly, Holly reached between them and positioned the thick cock at the entrance of her pussy. As she did so, she tried to wrap her hand all the way around his girth but she couldn't quite manage it.

Holly paused. God, he was big! Even bigger than she'd thought when she was feeling him through his trousers. What were the Anyone U Want people thinking making an android which such a huge piece of equipment? She didn't even know if she could handle it.

Somehow, the android Grant seemed to see the uncertainty on her face.

"Are you all right, sweetheart?" he asked tenderly, sweeping a strand of her long, auburn hair out of her eyes. "Having second thoughts?"

"No…no, I want you in me." Holly bit her lip. "It's just…"

"Yes?" he murmured and for a moment she could have sworn she saw genuine concern in his pale blue eyes.

"Well, it's just that they made you really, uh, *big* down there. And I haven't been with a guy in well…in years." She winced at the embarrassment of admitting this shameful fact. But then she took comfort in reminding herself that it was just an android she was talking to. "Anyway, I'm just not sure if I can, uh, take you," she finished, feeling foolish.

"You can take me," Grant assured her gently, stroking her cheek. "You're wet enough, sweetheart—we just have to take things slow."

"We...we do?" Holly was continually amazed at the workmanship that had gone into this android. How had the Anyone U Want engineers managed to make a machine that appeared to be so emotionally intelligent?

"We do," he murmured, leaning down to kiss her again. "So come on, Holly—open for me. Open up and let me own you."

The intense look in his eyes and his soft, low, commanding voice left her powerless to resist. With a little moan of pure submission, Holly spread her thighs even wider, welcoming him in, opening for the man she wanted more than she'd ever wanted anyone before.

"Slowly," Grant told her, nudging just the head of his broad shaft past her entrance. "So slowly, sweetheart."

Holly gasped as she felt another thick inch breech her opening and then another and another. God, he was so *big*—not just long but thick too! She wondered if she would be able to take him all.

"Are you all right?" he asked, watching her as he slipped slowly deeper. "Talk to me, Holly—let me know I'm not hurting you."

"You're...you're not hurting me," she whispered back breathlessly. There was a *little* pain as the massive shaft entered her, but it was more of a stretching feeling and in a way, it felt good. So good she closed her eyes for a moment and gave herself up to the sensation of being filled.

"No." Her boss's deep voice made Holly's eyes fly open. "No, look at me, Holly," he commanded softly. "I want to see it on your face when I slide inside you...want to see it in your eyes when I fuck your soft little cunt with my cock."

His hot, dirty words and the way he was holding her gaze was almost too much for Holly. He wasn't even all the way in but already she could feel her pleasure beginning to build again. Maybe it was the way he was looking at her or that soft, deep voice telling her exactly what he was going to do to her. Or maybe it was just the incredibly intimate feeling of being completely open for him—completely vulnerable as he filled her with himself.

At last, Holly felt him slip completely inside her, bottoming out inside her pussy.

"Oh!" she moaned as he made a deep noise of satisfaction.

"You feel that, sweetheart?" he murmured, thrusting just a little so that she moaned and wiggled under him. "That's me, all the way in you. That's me *owning* you right now."

"Grant..." He had her hands pinned over her head but Holly craned her neck, trying to kiss him. She knew it was pathetic but she couldn't help herself—she had genuine emotion coursing through her right now.

"Holly," he murmured and dropped his head to kiss her tenderly as his shaft pulled out and then thrust in again, bumping the end of her channel and making her cry out.

Grant swallowed her cries hungrily and then slid almost all the way out before thrusting in again—this time harder than before.

"*Oh!*" Holly wrapped her legs around his lean hips, urging him on. Now that she was used to his girth inside her, she found that she liked it—liked it a *lot*.

"That's right, sweetheart," he murmured in a low voice. "You're getting used to it now, aren't you? Getting used to being filled with my cock?"

"Y-yes," Holly admitted, bucking up to meet his next thrust. "I...I guess I am."

"That's good. Because this is where you belong, sweetheart—pinned under me, spread open with my cock inside you. This is where you've always belonged." Leaning down, he kissed her again, nipping lightly at her lips in a way that made her feel weak with need.

"I do?" she whispered as he thrust deep again—so deep she could feel the head of his cock kiss the mouth of her womb.

"You do," Grant affirmed, his eyes blazing into hers. "You're mine, Holly. *Mine*," he growled, pressing deep again—so deep it seemed like he was searching for her soul with each thrust. "Mine, now and forever. Now that I've claimed you, I'll never let you go."

Holly felt her eyes go wide at his words. God, he felt good inside her—just like he was meant to be there. Like they were meant to be together.

Stop thinking such crazy stuff—he's just an android, she tried to tell herself. But it was useless—Grant made it impossible to remember what he was. He looked into her eyes intently the whole time he was taking her, holding her gaze as he filled her with his thick shaft, owning her, making her his. Holly couldn't help falling into those icy-blue depths—in them it seemed she could feel all her common sense drowning.

But it wasn't just the way he was looking at her as he made love to her—the things he was saying...they were so shamelessly romantic. So completely unrealistic and yet so sweet she never wanted him to stop. Holly didn't know if she would ever be able to look her real boss in his eyes again, not after giving herself so completely, body and soul, to his android.

She closed her eyes for a moment, willing the emotion to go away but it wouldn't. And all the while the pleasure kept building and building until she thought she would die from the intensity of the impending orgasm.

"Look at me," Grant demanded again, making her open her eyes. "Are you close?"

"I...I am," she whispered." He wasn't pounding into her now—it was more of a slow, steady grind. He kept their bodies pressed together as he filled her, making short, deep thrusts so that the head of his cock kissed the mouth of her womb each time. The hard ridge of his pelvic bone was rubbing against her clit and his deep penetration was making Holly feel opened and owned in a way she hadn't even thought was possible. Just then he gave a particularly deep thrust and she moaned out loud. "Oh, Grant, I really am! *So close...*"

"That's good, sweetheart." He stroked her cheek, still holding her gaze intently. "Look at me, Holly. Look at me while you come," he ordered. "Come on my cock so I can fill you up completely."

Holly looked into his eyes and felt her heart swell even as a second, deeper orgasm started to shake her.

"Oh! Oh, *Grant!*" she cried as her toes curled and her back arched helplessly. She could feel her inner walls spasming around the thick invader of his cock as the warm tide of sensation washed over her, threatening to carry her away with the intensity of the pleasure coursing through her.

She held tight to Grant, her legs wrapped around his trim hips, her eyes locked with his as the orgasm shook her. She used him to anchor herself as the tidal wave of emotion and pleasure broke over her body and made her moan helplessly and call his name.

"Grant," she heard herself saying as he swelled even bigger within her and she felt the hot rush of his seed bathing her inner pussy. "Oh, Grant, I wish so much you were real!"

He released her hands and took her face in both of his big, warm palms.

"Holly," he said hoarsely, staring into her eyes. "Holly, I am real—all of this is *real.*"

Chapter Seven

At first his words didn't register. Holly just stared at him, thinking this must be a glitch in the programming. Some strange joke one of the engineers at Anyone U Want had put in, thinking it would be funny.

"But...but..." She looked uncertainly at the Grant android who was now claiming to be the real Grant. They were still joined together with his cock filling her pussy with his seed.

"It's real," he repeated. "This is real and I'm real, Holly. Not an android — this is the real me."

"But you...but I..." Holly's brain raced, remembering all the crazy, embarrassing words she'd been spouting — all the hidden confessions she'd been pouring out, thinking she was talking to an android. "You can't be real," she said at last. "I said...I said so many things because I thought..."

"I know what you thought," Grant said, looking at her intently. "Holly, I found your dream-viewer and I realized how you felt about me. So I decided —"

"You decided to violate my privacy and then invade my fantasy?" Holly demanded. She didn't know what was worse — that she'd given him her body so shamelessly or the fact that she'd bared her soul, spilling secrets she would have taken to her grave otherwise.

Grant frowned. "Holly, please. I never meant—"

"Get off me!" She shoved at him with both hands and he rose quickly but reluctantly, pulling out of her and allowing her to sit up.

Quickly, Holly shot off the desk and started pulling on her discarded clothes. She didn't know when she'd felt more betrayed. How could he do this to her? How could he pretend to be an android and let her tell him all her embarrassing feelings for him without saying a word? How could he let her make a complete and total fool out of herself?

"Holly..." Grant was up too and fastening his trousers. "Please, just listen."

"No, I'm through listening to you," she snapped. "And I'm through working for you, too. I want my return ticket to Earth. I'm *leaving*."

As she stormed out of area 25 of Anyone U Want, she dashed tears of anger and humiliation from her eyes. What a joke he must have thought her! How amusing to fulfill the fantasies of his poor, love-starved assistant.

He probably thought I would fall all over myself thanking him for being willing to lower himself to be with me, she thought. *That having one time with him would make me happy for life.*

Holly felt more than hurt—part of her felt broken. Humiliated beyond the ability to heal. Oh God, she just wanted to *die*. But she couldn't do that until she at least got back to Earth.

Over two hundred thousand miles from home and betrayed by the man she had idolized for the past two years, Holly had never felt more alone.

Chapter Eight

"Look, just *talk* to him—that's all I'm saying." Abby paced around their apartment, waving her arms. "It's been a week since you came back from the Moon and this is the third night in a row he's come up here wanting to speak to you." She peeked at the viewing-screen that served as a peephole and showed anyone outside their front door. Grant Harris the Third was standing there patiently, as though he could wear Holly down from sheer force of will.

"No." Holly looked away, determined not to be swayed by her friend's words.

"It looks like he's empty-handed tonight," Abby remarked, still watching Holly's ex-boss on the viewing-screen. "Maybe he got tired of you throwing his expensive gifts away."

The other two nights Grant had come, he'd brought things with him—a huge bouquet of flowers the first time and a box of expensive looking chocolates the second.

Not that Holly had taken the gifts. Abby had accepted them on her behalf and Holly had promptly thrown them down the waste chute. She made sure they landed in the dumpster near the parking area, so he could see exactly what she thought of his presents—and what she thought of him.

"Okay, you don't have to talk to him but you do have to tell me—*what happened on that business trip?*" Abby looked at her intently. "Come on, Holly, what did he do? Sexually harass you?"

"Not *exactly.*" Holly was still far too mortified to explain to her best friend what had happened. How could she admit she'd blown all her available cash on a fantasy with an android that looked like her boss, only to find out that it *was* actually her boss she was having sex with? It was all just too weird and complicated and she didn't want to have to deal with it. She didn't want to have to deal with Grant Harris the Third either, but he was apparently a persistent son-of-a-bitch. When would he leave her alone?

The doorbell chimed out the latest hot little pop song… and then chimed again and again and again. Holly frowned in annoyance and looked up to see what was going on in the viewing-screen.

Grant was leaning on the bell—literally pressing it non-stop and making the tinkly little tune Abby had programmed into it play over and over until Holly thought she would go crazy.

"Open the door," she told Abby. "Tell him to leave or we'll call the cops."

"What?" Abby gasped. "You can't do that! He's Grant Harris the Third—he can do anything he wants."

"Not with our doorbell he can't." Holly felt all the rage and humiliation she'd suffered suddenly boiling up to the surface. She might be mild-mannered and tame most of the time but not now—not after what Grant had done.

Finally angry enough to confront her ex-boss, she marched to the door and threw it open.

"What?" she demanded. *"Do…you…want?"*

"To talk to you." He glared at her, his ice-blue eyes as cold as glaciers. "I have a lot to say to you that you wouldn't listen to last time we were in the same room together."

"Last time we were in the same room together you impersonated an android and spanked me and had sex with me!" Holly flared.

"What?" Abby was suddenly there, her eyes wide with interest.

"None of your business," Holly elbowed her hard. "Look, could you *please* just go back to your bedroom and let me get this over with?"

"I have a better idea," Grant said smoothly. He snapped his fingers and a handsome chauffer wearing a black suit appeared. "Forsythe, would you be so kind as to take Miss Sparks' roommate somewhere and buy her anything she wants?"

"Certainly, Sir." The handsome chauffer gave Abby a knowing grin. "Are you more interested in fur or diamonds?"

"Neither," said Abby, frowning loyally. "I'm not going anywhere."

Grant sighed. "If your refusal to go is because you're afraid I'll hurt Holly, please be assured I won't lay a hand on her. But I cannot go until I talk to her and I cannot talk to her unless we have some *privacy*."

"Well..." Abby looked uncertainly at Holly who sighed.

"Fine. Just go. He's not going to get the message until I tell him to his face, I guess." She glared up at Grant who put his best blank face on and stared back.

"Oh, goody!" Abby jumped forward and tucked her arm through the chauffer's. "Now what were you saying earlier about diamonds and furs? Or maybe a nice new hovercar?"

The chauffer grinned and they walked down the apartment hallway together without a second glance for Holly or Grant. Holly watched them go with a frown. Great, now she was all alone with her ex-boss. Well, might as well get this over with.

She put a hand on her hip and looked up at him.

"Fine. You got rid of my friend—happy?"

"I will be if you invite me in and listen to what I have to say," Grant said mildly. "Please, Holly, just *listen*."

"Holly, is it? What happened to 'Miss Sparks?' and 'Mr. Harris'?"

"I think we're beyond that now, don't you?" he asked quietly. "Now will you please let me in and listen to what I have to say?"

Holly had a very strong desire to tell him to go screw himself but she realized that until Grant had his say, he wouldn't leave her alone. She'd seen his dogged persistence often enough in the years that she worked for him—it often worked in his favor when he was doing a particularly complicated business deal.

Well it won't work in his favor now, she told herself grimly as she stood aside and finally let him into her small apartment.

"Thank you," Grant said with quiet gravity. "This is...nice. A nice place you have here."

"Welcome to how the other half lives," Holly said, shutting the door behind him with a bang. "We can't all afford trips to the moon and caviar for lunch."

"You couldn't exactly afford to rent that android at Anyone U Want either but you did anyway," he pointed out softly.

Holly felt her cheeks go hot and red but she lifted her chin and refused to drop her eyes.

"What I decided to do with my Christmas bonus was my *private* choice," she said clearly. "And it was my privacy that you invaded — among other things."

To her surprise, Grant didn't try to argue.

"You're right," he said softly. "What I did was unforgivable and I have no excuse."

"Well, we certainly agree on that," Holly snapped. "So is that all you have to say?"

"No." He frowned down at her and she wished she were taller. "No, I felt like there is…unfinished business between us."

"Unfinished business?" Holly looked at him, uncomprehending. Then suddenly, it came to her what he must mean. "I'm not pregnant, if that's what you're worried about," she said, crossing her arms over her chest. "So don't worry—your life isn't going to turn into some cheesy romance—*The Billionaire's Secret Baby*—or anything like that."

"Pregnant?" He frowned. "I never even...I suppose I should have but I never even considered that."

"And I don't want to sue you for sexual harassment either," Holly continued relentlessly. "That would mean letting everyone in the world know what a stupid fool I made of myself, once the press got hold of the story. I have no interest in going there."

"Holly, you didn't make a fool of yourself," he protested, his deep voice sounding tired. "*I* was the one who acted like a fool."

"Oh? That's not how I see it." She put one hand on her hip. "You weren't the one who paid for an android that looked like your boss to sex you up. God, I'm such an idiot! I should have known when you started going off script that you weren't really an android. But I just thought..."

"You thought what?" he asked softly.

"I thought...I *knew* a man like you wouldn't be interested in me," she flared back. "That's why I should have known something wasn't right."

"Why would you think that?" he demanded.

"Well, because…look at you." Holly gestured at him. "You date supermodels."

"No I don't," he countered quickly. "Not anymore. In fact, not for the past year and a half since I started paying attention to you."

"What?" Holly raised her eyebrows. "What are you talking about?"

"I'm talking about the fact that I wanted you every bit as much as you wanted me." He sounded frustrated now. "But I thought I couldn't have you—I told myself you were off limits."

"Because I'm poor and common and I don't wear a size two?" she demanded. "Because your family wouldn't approve?"

"As a matter of fact, they *wouldn't* approve but I don't give a damn about that—I don't give a damn about any of it," Grant growled. "The reason I told myself you were off limits was because I have certain…sexual tastes I thought would frighten you. But then I saw all the things you had on your dream-viewer."

"Oh God, did you see *everything?*" Holly felt herself wilting inside with mortification. She had some really extreme fantasies in there. God, this was so *embarrassing!*

"I saw enough to give me hope," Grant said soberly. "And then I saw the brochure from Anyone U Want. I was excited — finally it seemed like everything I wanted — like *you*, Holly — were within my grasp. And so..." He took a deep breath. "And so I did something very stupid and ill conceived."

"You paid the Anything U Want people to take the android's place," Holly said flatly. She still didn't believe a word he said about wanting her for over a year. Oh she wanted to believe — wanted desperately to think this could be true. But part of her whispered that it couldn't be real. That Grant was probably just here to do damage control.

"Yes." Grant let out a deep sigh. "In retrospect, I shouldn't have done that. I should have waited and asked you out on a date instead of...doing what I did."

"Just say it," Holly snapped. "Instead of giving me the best sex of my life and then bringing the truth crashing down on my head."

Grant looked intrigued. "Was it really the best? It was for me, too."

His words made her embarrassment flare all over again.

"Okay, you've had your say — now you can go." Holly made a motion towards the door.

"What? Why?" He looked really upset now. "Don't you believe me when I tell you I want you?"

"No," Holly said bluntly. "I think you're just here to smooth things over so I won't sue you or file rape charges or anything like that. Well don't worry, Grant—that's not me."

"I know that's not you," he said quietly. "I know you, Holly—I know what makes you tick. I know what you want…and how you need to submit."

His words made her heart pound but Holly refused to let it show on her face.

"Funnily enough, I'm not feeling very submissive just now," she said in as cold a tone as she could manage. "So why don't you leave me alone?"

* * * * *

Grant stared at her in frustration. How could he get it across to her how he felt? How could he get her to listen to him?

"Holly," he said in a low, even voice. "You're the only woman I have been interested in for the last year and a half—longer than that, if I'm honest with myself. And when I found out you shared my sexual interests, well, I couldn't help myself. I *had* to have you."

"Stop it!" she snapped, her pale cheeks flaming red. "It's not like I'm the only girl in the world who has submissive fantasies. You're Grant Harris the Third—you could have anyone you wanted."

"But the only one I want is *you*." He took a step forward, praying she would listen. He cupped her red cheek in one hand and was encouraged when she didn't pull back. "I heard your friend, Abby, saying that I came empty-handed tonight," he murmured, looking into her eyes. "Because I didn't bring chocolates or flowers."

"I don't want your gifts," Holly protested, but her voice was slightly breathless and she still wasn't pulling away from his touch. Was she finally beginning to believe him?"

"The thing is—I *didn't* come empty-handed," Grant told her. "I realized what empty, meaningless gestures flowers and candy are. And so…I brought you this instead."

Reaching into his pocket, he pulled out a small, velvet box and dropped to one knee in front of her.

Holly's eyes got huge when he lifted the lid, revealing the 14 carat, rose-gold, oval-cut Morganite diamond ring.

"G-grant?" she stuttered, almost unable to get his name out.

"Holly," he murmured, taking her hand. "You're the only woman in the world for me. I mean it."

"I...I don't know what to say." Holly looked at him, her eyes shining. "You're serious? *Really serious?*"

"I've never been more serious about anything in my life." Grant rose and pulled her close, looking down into her big, lovely eyes. "I want to be your husband...and your Dominant, Holly. Will you marry me?"

"I...I..." For a moment he thought she was going to say no and his heart stuttered in his chest. But then she threw her arms around his neck—standing on her tiptoes to do so—and hugged him tight. "Yes," she whispered. "If you really mean it then yes—I'll marry you."

More relieved than he could say, Grant pulled her close and took her mouth in a hungry kiss. She tasted every bit as good as he remembered and felt just as soft and perfect in his arms. Let other men drool over skinny, vapid supermodels without a brain in their heads—he had Holly. His wonderful, intelligent, hot-blooded Holly and he was never letting her go.

Holly pulled out of the kiss at last and looked up at him, her eyes shining. Then she pinched his cheek as hard as she could.

"Ouch!" Grant looked at her uncertainly. "Why did you do that?"

"Just making sure you're not an android," she said, smiling sweetly. "After all, you can't be too sure."

"I assure you I'm absolutely real and I will absolutely give you the spanking of your life for being rude to your Dom, sweetheart," he growled softly.

Holly's eyes widened and he thought he felt her heartbeat quicken, crushed as she was against him.

"Why, Mr. Harris...are you going to *spank* me?" she breathed.

Grant grinned and put a proprietary hand on her full ass.

"Let's just see, Miss Sparks. Let's just see..."

The End

Do you like scorching romance, heart-pounding adventure, and hot sex in your sci-fi? Then try Evangeline's Best Selling Brides of the Kindred series. The first book, <u>Claimed</u>*, is absolutely FREE. Start the saga today...*

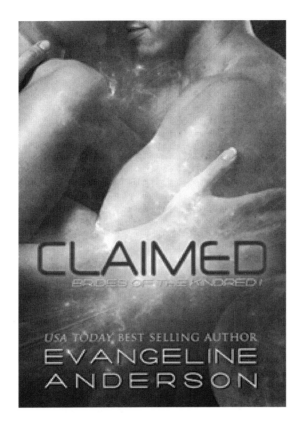

Brides of the Kindred book 1: <u>Claimed</u>

Prologue

Dusk was falling on Idlewild Avenue. Rows of identical townhouses, lit softly from within, lined the street which was overshadowed by huge old oak trees. A light evening shower had just passed and now the atmosphere was heavy with moisture. Tendrils of steam rose from the asphalt and the sweet scent of honeysuckle filled the air.

In number eleven at the end of the row a slender female figure moved in front of a large picture window — one of the selling points of the otherwise unremarkable houses. She was walking back and forth, placing objects on a table, or perhaps taking them away — maybe cleaning up after dinner. She moved with ease and grace as she did the mundane chore, completely unaware that she was being watched.

Across the road from the lighted window and the slender figure, two pairs of eyes looked on avidly as she moved. One set of eyes was a pale, piercing blue that was almost white and the other set was a warm amber-gold that wouldn't have looked out of place in the face of a tiger.

Neither pair of eyes was human.

"Mine." The low rumbling growl came from the owner of the amber eyes. He was tall, six foot seven at least, with shoulders so broad he would have to turn sidewise to go through most doorways, but he moved silently, with a feral grace that belied his muscular physique. Dark stubble covered his cheeks and chin and matched the thick black hair on his head.

"Not yet, Baird," the one beside him cautioned. He was as tall as his friend and just as muscular but he had short, spiky blond hair that complimented his pale blue eyes.

"Can't wait much longer." Long, strong fingers curled into a fist as though the amber-eyed male could grasp the slender figure in his hand and hold her through sheer force of will. "Been dreaming about her every night, Sylvan. I ache for her."

"What does she look like?" There was genuine curiosity in the question. Though Baird had never seen her outside his dreams, Sylvan had no doubt he could describe his chosen female to the last detail.

"So fuckin' beautiful it hurts to look at her. Yellow hair like yours but longer — more golden. And her eyes..." Baird shook his head. "Like jewels. A pale grey that's almost silver."

"You find these human women appealing then?"

"Only her — she's the only one I can see." The amber eyes stared hungrily across the road. "I need her soon. Need to be with her. In her."

"You're sure she's the one?" Sylvan stared doubtfully at the woman silhouetted in the window. She was humming softly to herself but despite the distance and the pane of glass between them he could hear her perfectly and knew Baird could too. As attuned as his half brother was to this human female, he could probably hear her heartbeat even from across the street.

"I *know* she's the one." There wasn't a shred of doubt in the deep, rumbling voice. "Didn't I tell you we've been dream-sharing? And her scent..." He inhaled deeply and his dark gold eyes were suddenly half-lidded with desire. "It's her all right and she's ripe for bonding. I want her."

"I know you do, but Baird..." The other male shifted from foot to foot uneasily. "You haven't been back that long—only three days and it's a miracle you escaped alive. Don't you think it might be a good idea to wait a while? To take some time to recover?"

"Waited long enough," was the rumbling reply. "Six months in that hell hole and the only thing keeping me alive and sane were the dreams I had of her. I won't wait any longer—she's mine, whether she knows it yet or not."

"You'll scare her," his half-brother objected. "Human women are frightened enough of us as it is."

"I won't hurt her. Just need to take her—bond her." Unconsciously, he took a step toward the lighted window but his half-brother put a restraining hand on his broad shoulder.

"Wait." The other male's voice was soothing. "Just wait until they serve the papers. One more night and she's yours but you can't have her now—not without violating the contract."

A low, frustrated growl was his answer as the thick muscles of Baird's upper arms bunched with tension.

"Come on." The one called Sylvan tugged his half brother gently away from the lighted window. "If you stay here you'll do something you regret. Remember, just one more night."

The other male stood like a rock for a moment despite his brother's tugging. Then, reluctantly, he allowed himself to be led away. He cast one last possessive glance over his shoulder at the figure in the window.

"Mine," he repeated with unshakable certainty. "Mine whether you know it or not, *Lilenta*. And tomorrow I claim you."

Chapter One

"Bad dreams again last night?"

Olivia Waterhouse jerked at the sound of her twin sister's voice and then went back to staring at the kitchen table. "Uh, not so much," she lied and tried to smile.

"C'mon, Liv, give. It's me, your womb mate — remember?" Sophia sat down across from her and patted her hand gently. No one could ever decide if the Waterhouse twins were fraternal or identical. Liv had honey blonde hair with grey eyes and Sophia had a rich, chestnut mane with pale green eyes but their facial features were exactly the same. They had the same build too, both were five-seven and slender with hourglass curves. More than just twins, they were also best friends, which was why it made Liv uncomfortable to lie to her sister. But she couldn't help it — the things she'd seen last night didn't bear repeating.

"Really," she said, not meeting her sister's eyes. "I'm fine. I just had a restless night — that's all."

The truth was the dreams she'd been having for the past half year about the muscular stranger with glowing, amber-gold eyes had become progressively more disturbing. He was her nighttime visitor every time she closed her eyes. Liv had even named him — inside her head she called him "the dark man."

For the longest time she'd dreamed of him someplace filled with shadows — someplace where despair was an almost palpable thing. Sometimes he was chained to the wall, his head bowed as if in exhaustion. Other times were worse. Liv had seen him hooked to some kind of machine, wires embedded in his dusky tan skin like malignant snakes feeding off him. On an inverted dome, as big as an IMAX screen above his head, images flashed — pictures of strange worlds she never could have imagined. One seemed to be all ice and snow, another a lush tropical jungle where the vegetation was mostly blue instead of green. And yet another seemed to be a world that was mostly a clear, golden ocean with tiny rocky islands dotted here and there.

When she dreamed of the pictures of other worlds flashing across the enormous screen, Liv always got the idea that they were somehow drawn from the memories of the dark man. And there was pain — so much pain, both physical and emotional. He was hurting and she was powerless to help him. She didn't even know him but somehow his agony affected her deeply. She woke up with tears in her eyes most mornings, her heart clenched like a fist in her chest, his name — a name she could never quite recall — trembling on her lips.

Liv tried to tell herself her dreams were just that — only dreams. Lots of people had reoccurring dreams. Why her brain should choose to show her the same thing night after night was a mystery but it was also no big deal. And she only felt for the mysterious dark man because that was the kind of person she was. She'd just finished nursing school a few weeks ago and was taking some time off before she started her new job in the pediatric unit at Tampa General. She could be tough when she had to but by nature she was a nurturing person. Otherwise she wouldn't care how this man, this dream stranger, was hurting. Wouldn't care about the pain she saw in his unusual amber eyes.

Then, two or three nights ago, the dreams had changed. When she finally let herself sleep, she saw the man as usual but he was free. Unchained and out of the shadowy place where his only emotions had been despair and agony.

The change in her depressing dream should have elated Liv but she found herself frightened instead. Because in her new dreams the huge man with black hair and golden eyes was looking for someone — searching tirelessly. And somehow she knew that the person he was searching for was *her*.

Then last night, he'd found her. Liv still remembered sitting bolt upright in bed at four in the morning, her hand pressed between her breasts as if to still her pounding heart. The scene in the dream had showed the mysterious dark man staring right into her eyes and he's spoken only one word.

"Mine."

"What?" Sophia looked at her in concern and Liv realized she'd quoted her dream aloud.

"Nothing. What's for breakfast?" It was a Saturday morning — the day officially decreed as off the diet and anything goes. Liv tried to curb herself the rest of the week — her curvy figure was already a lot more hippy than she liked — but on Saturday she let herself off the leash.

"How about pancakes? Kat's coming over and bringing some blueberries from that organic farmer's market on Dunn. Sound good?"

"Mmm." Liv nodded, trying to look enthusiastic and failing miserably if the expression on her twin's face was any indication.

"Come on, Liv, blueberry pancakes are your favorite." Sophia frowned as she moved around the warm yellow and cream kitchen, getting out the eggs and flour and sugar and pulling down a frying pan from the hanging rack above the sink.

"Yummy. Can't wait." Liv gave her a weak smile and stifled a yawn. "Seriously, Sophie, I'm just tired. I stayed up a little too late reading."

Sophia shot her a skeptical look. "Right. And that's why you look like one of my first graders who's just been sent to the principal's office." She taught at an affluent private school in South Tampa that catered to the wealthy and gifted children of the city and she absolutely loved her job. Since it was summer, however, she had three months off to pursue her other love — art.

Liv knew Sophia was itching to go paint and was probably only hanging around the kitchen making blueberry pancakes because she was worried about her twin. She opened her mouth to protest that she was fine again when a *rat-a-tat-tat* sounded at their front door.

"Coming!" Sophia beat her to the door and opened it to the beaming face of Katrina O'Connor, their mutual friend since high school. As Sophia ushered Kat inside, Liv shook herself mentally. It was time she stopped letting these silly dreams affect her so much. She was Olivia Waterhouse and she wasn't afraid of anything.

Despite being compassionate Liv was no pushover. She had worked her way through nursing school and always stood up for herself, even to the crankiest doctors who could verbally eviscerate anyone with a sarcastic word or two. She went car shopping and to the mechanic by herself and never got screwed over. And most importantly, she never took no for an answer — when she really wanted something, she went for it. So why was she letting a stupid dream put a crimp in her personal style?

Time to get over it, girl, she lectured herself sternly. *It's just a dream and he's not real. Let it go and enjoy your pancakes. It's a beautiful Saturday — anything could happen.* But rather than cheering her up, the thought sent a shiver down her spine. *That's right anything could happen…anything at all.*

"What's your deal, Liv? You look like you saw a ghost." Kat's cheery voice broke her morbid train of thought and Liv looked up and tried to smile.

"Hey, Kat-woman. Heard you were bringing some blueberries."

"Did better than that." Kat put a large recycled cloth shopping bag on the round kitchen table and started pulling things out of it, like a magician pulling rabbits out of a hat. "Eggs, butter, ham, chives…" She stopped to push a wisp of auburn hair behind her ear before continuing. "Some fresh shitake mushrooms, goat cheese — "

"Whoa — whoa!" Liv was startled into laughing. "What the hell kind of pancakes are we making here, anyway?"

"Not pancakes — quiche. I saw this new recipe last night on Food Network — "

Liv and Sophia both groaned aloud at this, cutting her off. Kat was a paralegal at Linden and James downtown but she had always had grand aspirations when it came to cooking. Unfortunately, she didn't like to follow a recipe so most of her culinary creations landed in the trash—a fact that didn't discourage her in the least when it came to trying something new. Especially if she was working in someone else's kitchen and didn't have to worry about cleaning up the mess afterwards.

"Tell me something, Kat," Sophia demanded. "Exactly how much of that stuff in the bag does the recipe call for?"

"And how much is your own addition?" Liv finished her twin's thought effortlessly.

"Come on, you guys." Kat pouted unconvincingly. "This one is going to be good, I can tell. And just because it doesn't actually *call* for sardines and black olives doesn't mean they won't be good in there."

"Black olives?" Sophia made a face.

"And sardines? Yuck! Are you making a quiche or an everything pizza?" Liv crossed her arms over her chest.

Kat noticed the gesture and grinned. "Ooo, nice nighty, Liv. Did we have a nocturnal visitor last night?"

Liv opened her mouth but Sophia beat her to it. "No one besides her dream man—whoever he is."

"I didn't dream about him last night," Liv lied defensively. "And I wore this because I happen to like it—it's comfortable." In contrast to Sophie's Sesame Street pjs and Kat's sensible t-shirt and shorts, she had on her lacy black baby doll nighty. It was the one her ex fiancé, Mitch had given her and it had a short black robe and panties that matched.

Liv wasn't wearing the set because she missed the jerk—she'd really dodged a bullet when she gave him back his ring and told him to hit the road. It was more a case of not letting something so nice go to waste. Mitch may have been a cheating bastard but he had good taste in underwear—underwear for her, anyway. He'd worn tighty-whities himself. Liv had always struggled not to laugh when he strutted around the house in them, thinking he looked so hot.

"She *claims* she stayed up late reading a book—that's why the dark circles and eye luggage." Sophia sounded skeptical.

"Well you look like hell," Kat said frankly. "It must have been some book. Was it a horror novel or what?"

"Something like that," Liv muttered sulkily. She was in no mood to put up with her friend's teasing.

"Well don't get bent out of shape, doll." Kat smiled at her as she continued pulling ingredients out of her shopping bag. Liv hoped the strawberries and mangos were for a fruit salad and not the sardine and black olive quiche. "I just thought with that sexy outfit maybe you'd finally decided to get back on the dating train. You and Mitch hit splitsville over six months ago now."

"You're the last one to talk about dating." Sophia was whisking something in a bowl—no doubt she'd decided to make pancake batter after all as a back up to the disastrous quiche. "You're even worse with men than me—and I *suck* at the social scene," she added, tasting the batter and reaching for a bottle of vanilla extract.

"Exactly—because most men today don't appreciate the pleasures of a plus sized woman." Kat gestured at her own lush figure with a small pineapple she'd pulled out of the seemingly bottomless bag. "Which is why I have to live vicariously through you two skinny-minnies. A size eight looks good in that naughty little nighty—a size eighteen, not so much."

It was true Kat was a size eighteen but she had it all in the right places, Liv thought. She had often wished that her breasts were as full as Kat's but then, Kat was full to running over all over the place, including her mouth. She was thinking of going back to school to become a lawyer instead of just a paralegal because getting paid to argue was her idea of a perfect job. Usually her quick wit and naughty sense of humor cracked Liv up but this morning she *so* wasn't in the mood.

"Change the subject. Preferably away from my hot jammies and the fact that I don't have a man to wear them for," she said, getting up from the table and going to the fridge for a glass of juice. Actually she'd tried dating again after she'd dumped Mitch but somehow it didn't feel right. Mainly because none of the men she went out with were tall and dark with glowing amber eyes...*Stop that!* she scolded herself, pulling open the fridge door which was covered in colorful magnets and reaching for the carton of OJ. *Stop thinking about him — he's not even real!*

She tried concentrating on her favorite fridge magnet instead, the one with two California rolls in bed side by side. The caption underneath read, *Wake up, little sushi!*

"Okay, sourpuss, try this subject on for size," Kat snapped, folding the empty shopping bag and stowing it away in her barn-sized purse. "You remember Jillian Holms that took home-ec with us in high school?"

"The head cheerleader?" Sophia made a face. "How could we forget?"

"That's her." Kat nodded enthusiastically. "Well, you're not going to believe this but she got drafted."

There was complete silence in the room for about two seconds and then Liv and Sophia said simultaneously, "She *what?*"

"Got drafted. I know, can you even believe it?"

There was no need to ask what Kat meant when she said their old acquaintance from Hillsborough High had gotten drafted—every woman in the room knew about the draft and every one of them lived in fear of it.

Five years before the Earth had been suddenly attacked. The space station orbiting the moon, which had been completed in 2025, had been destroyed and the rest of the planet was threatened by a mysterious force known only as the Scourge. Attempts to contact and reason with the menacing threat had failed and even the deadliest weapons had little or no effect. It looked like the Earth was down for the count and everyone on the planet was going to wind up as alien take-out.

Liv remembered those horrible days—it had been forty-eight hours of mass panic. Suicides, bombings, looting and unprotected sex which she thankfully had not personally participated in. With no other immediate family, she and Sophie and Kat had locked the doors to the little apartment she'd been living in at the time and eaten themselves sick on

Ben and Jerry's while they watched a never-ending marathon of vintage chick flicks.

It might not have been the most productive way to spend their last days on Earth but eating your body weight in Chunky Monkey and watching *Sixteen Candles* and *Pretty Woman* beat chowing down on the business end of a gun or having sex with a total stranger any day of the week, in Liv's opinion. And their wait-and-see approach had been justified — in the end everything turned out all right.

Because of the Kindred.

The Kindred were a race of alien warriors, humanoid in form but much more massive in scale than the average human male. They had swooped in suddenly and forced the Scourge to stop their attack and retreat to the far side of the moon. There were rumors that the war continued somewhere in space with scrimmages and battles between the two factions but if so, it was kept quiet. The alien warriors took up orbit around the planet, ensuring that the tenuous peace continued, for Earth at least. And they only wanted one thing in exchange — a genetic trade.

Because a mutation in their genes caused their race to be ninety-five percent male, the Kindred had become a space faring race, looking for other planets to inhabit and other humanoid species to trade with. Earth was only the fourth planet in their ten thousand year odyssey to offer a viable trade and they were eager to get started.

Of course the governments of Earth agreed to the trade — what else could they do? The only thing that stood between the planet and total annihilation was the warrior race keeping watch far above the ionosphere, so it was considered best to keep them happy. An all female draft was set up which every unmarried woman between the ages of nineteen and thirty-five was required to enter. It was considered a patriotic duty but also a long shot. There was only about a one in ten thousand chance of ever getting called to do your "duty" which was why it was so unusual to actually know a person who'd been drafted.

The Kindred pretty much kept to themselves, staying in their ships above the surface of the planet and only coming down occasionally in twos and threes to claim their brides. Nobody knew how they picked them and personally, Liv didn't want to know. It was easier to pretend that the Kindred didn't exist, easier to forget that you personally might win the bed-an-alien lottery at any minute. But something like this — actually knowing a girl who'd been drafted — made pretending and forgetting impossible.

"So what exactly happened?" Sophie had stopped whisking her batter, intent on Kat's latest piece of news.

Liv realized she was still gripping the juice carton with the fridge door open. She shut the door and turned around. "Yeah, what happened?" She couldn't help echoing her twin's question.

Kat shrugged. "Two draft officers came to her house and took her down to the HKR building. Then she had to sign some kind of a contract—like a marriage license I think." There was a Human/Kindred Relations building in every major city in the world built specifically for this purpose but Liv had never been inside the Tampa facility which was located downtown. Just driving by it gave her the willies so she tried not to even look at it when she did.

"What…which kind of Kindred did she get?" Sophia asked in a hushed voice. The Kindred were split into three distinct branches, all outcomes of their past genetic trades.

There were the Tranq Kindred—a group of males with piercing blue eyes and a double set of short, sharp vestigial fangs. There were rumors that the fangs grew and they bit when they had sex with the female of their choice and other rumors that they could heal any illness with a bite. Liv wasn't sure how much of that was true and how much was just media hype but the buzz about their sexual habits had earned this group the nickname "Blood Kindred."

Then there were the Twins, a branch of the Kindred in which the males always came in pairs and had to share a woman. No one knew exactly why and they declined to offer an explanation. Some said they were telepathic and needed sex to communicate but that hadn't been proven—not that anyone had ever gotten a chance to study them. The Kindred as a whole kept strictly to themselves and refused to participate in any kind of scientific research or experiments. So no one really knew anything about the Twin Kindred other than they refused to make love to a woman individually.

And then there were the Ragers—also known as the Beast Kindred.

Working for so long in a hospital as she went through nursing school, the sight and idea of drawing blood wasn't frightening to Liv so the Blood Kindred didn't scare her. And being a twin herself, she wasn't terribly afraid of the Twin Kindred either. But the Beast Kindred, well…they scared the ever-loving crap out of her.

As tall and dominant as the rest of the warrior race, the Beast Kindred were said to have the most unpredictable tempers. Rumor had it that they could go into berserker-like rages when protecting their women, killing anyone that stood in their way no matter how many opposed them. But it was the other rumors, the sexual rumors, which put a lump in Liv's throat.

Besides being filled with animalistic lust, the Beast Kindred were said to have sexual stamina unequaled by anyone. Rumor had it that they could come again and again without going soft and their marathon love-making sessions put even practitioners of tantric sex to shame.

Just the idea of being held in place, helpless, while a huge alien male filled her for hours made Liv's blood run cold. She hadn't had many lovers but the men she'd been with in the past had convinced her that sex was like a box of chocolates—you never knew what you were going to get when you went to bed with a man. And sadly, you were more likely to pick the nasty pink marshmallow cream than the yummy nut cluster. So rather than lingering for an indefinite amount of time, it was better to get in, get out, and get on with your life. Cuddling was more fun in the long run anyway.

The year and a half she'd spent with Mitch had only reinforced her ideas. In retrospect, Liv couldn't understand why she'd stayed with him so long. His idea of good sex was to get on top and grind her into the mattress while chanting, "Who's your daddy? Who's your daddy?" over and over again until she wanted to scream and *not* in a good way. No amount of tactful hints that references to her parentage during intimate encounters didn't do a thing for her would make him stop. Finally Liv had given up and just plugged her tiny iPod micro-mini into her ear whenever it looked like he wanted some nooky. She'd even had a playlist called "sex with Mitch."

That had been bad enough but at least Mitch had never had the stamina to get through the whole playlist. Liv imagined with horror what it would be like to have sex with a man who could go through the entire micro on shuffle setting without quitting once. Just the thought was enough to send her running—which was why the idea of getting chosen by a Beast Kindred freaked her out completely.

Don't they say the Beast Kindred have golden eyes? whispered a small voice in her head. *Shut up!* Liv told it fiercely. *He's just a dream and that's all there is to it.*

"So what kind did she get?" she forced herself to ask, not looking at Kat while she got a glass from the cabinet.

"Twins, I think." Kat shivered. "Can you even imagine? I mean, I know lots of people have had three-ways. You get drunk in college and before you know it you're getting the shaft, both literally and figuratively. But two horny frat guys is one thing—the Kindred are supposed to be hung like *Clydesdales.*"

"Kat!" Sophie slapped at her with the hand not holding the bowl full of pancake batter. "You are so bad!"

"But I mean honestly, how would they *fit*? You'd be bowlegged for life if you ended up with a pair of Twin Kindred." Kat raised her eyebrows comically and took a few wincing steps as though it hurt to walk. Sophie giggled and shook her head. Liv tried but all she could manage was a weak smile as she poured the orange juice and put the carton back in the fridge.

"Well, I hope she's happy. When does she come back?"

"She's not. She did her month and she's staying." Kat went back to assembling her quiche ingredients which appeared to include fresh thyme, basil, and cilantro as well as some cayenne pepper. "You know everyone that gets drafted has to sign an agreement to at least try things out for that long—a month long claiming period. After that you can come back and call it quits for good—*if* you and the Kindred stud who chose you haven't made the beast with two backs. If you have…" She shrugged fatalistically. "Well then it's too bad for you. You're a Kindred bride for life and they don't do divorce or separation. So it looks like Jillian's stuck"

"How do you know so much about it?" Liv demanded.

"I helped one of our attorneys prepare a case for some clients of my firm. We had this young woman's family try to sue when she got called up," Kat said matter-of-factly.

"What were the grounds?" Sophie asked.

"That she was a virgin and wasn't prepared to be with, uh, such a large guy." Kat snickered. "But all I have to say is, sitting there, listening to what this huge masculine alien could and couldn't do to you sexually and what *you* could and couldn't to do to *him* with your parents listening in *had* to be at least as bad as actually doing it."

"How embarrassing!" Sophie shuddered. "I'd rather die."

"Did they win the case?" Liv asked, taking a sip of juice.

Kat shook her head. "Not on your life. The court threw it out almost before her lawyer finished talking. Everybody knows we have to keep the Kindred happy. The Scourge is still out there somewhere and if throwing the big guys a bone by boning them is the only way to keep them on our side, well then, so be it. So if you get drafted you better develop a taste for alien nookie pretty quick."

"You know the thing that really freaks me out?" Sophie dropped the blueberries into the batter, stirring as she talked. "The fact that nobody ever decides to leave and go back to their old life after that initial thirty day period is up. You can't tell me the Kindred always know *exactly* which woman is going to be their soul mate for life when they pick a bride."

Kat shrugged and started cracking eggs into a large mixing bowl. "Maybe they brainwash you once you get up to their ship. Maybe it's filled with all kinds of sex toys and pleasure rooms and it's so good you just can't say no."

"Or maybe they trick you into having sex in the first place—like they slip you a roofie," Sophie said darkly. "And when you wake up it's like, 'Oh, sorry—we did the deed and now you're mine for life. Hope you don't mind moving to a galaxy far, far away and having sixteen pound alien babies the rest of your natural.'"

Liv gripped her glass full of OJ tightly. This certainly wasn't the first time they'd speculated about the Kindred when they got together on a girls' day but for some reason her nerves were so on edge she felt like she might scream if she had to listen to another word. Just then the doorbell chimed faintly and she breathed a sigh of relief—finally a distraction.

"I'll get it!" She was already halfway to the door when Sophia objected.

"Liv, you're hardly decent! That outfit almost shows your panties."

"I'm fine," Liv called back, pulling the short black lace robe that went with her baby doll nighty more tightly around her. "It's probably just Mrs. Jensen from next door. She's always wanting to borrow something—eggs, sugar, you name it."

She threw open the door expecting to see the kind and wrinkled face of her next door neighbor and instead was treated to the sight of two perfectly huge males in black uniforms.

"I...I...Who are you?" Liv gasped, barely able to get the words out.

"H/K officers Trex and Locan at your service," the one on the right rumbled and both of them made stiff, abbreviated bows. "We're here for Miss Olivia Lauren Waterhouse." He held up a digital picture and Liv recognized her own face staring back from the holo sheet. "This is you—correct?"

"I...yes, that's me," she said weakly, meaning both the picture and the name.

"And can you sign this document, verifying that it is so?" He held out a thick sheaf of papers with legal looking words on them along with a pen. Liv signed automatically where he indicated.

"All right, but I—" she began as the guard snatched back the papers and stuffed them into his uniform pocket.

"Excellent. Subject confirms identity," said the one on the left, as though he was making some kind of official report. "Preparing to escort subject to the HKR building at once." As one, both huge officers stepped forward and each took one of her elbows. The glass full of orange juice dropped from her fingers and shattered on the tile of the foyer like a bomb, spraying glass shards and sticky juice everywhere. One shard pieced her heel when she took a step back but Liv barely noticed the sharp little pain.

"Now wait just a minute," she protested, aware that both Sophia and Kat had crowded into the doorway behind her. "What are you saying? Where are you taking me? And can't I change first?"

"Negative. Flight risk is incurred if the subject is allowed to linger on the premises for any reason," barked the one on the right.

"But I haven't done anything. Let me go!" Liv struggled against them but it was like she was being held in pincers of iron on either side.

Kat and Sophie were suddenly there in front of the huge males, blocking their exit. It was like two Toy Poodles facing off Great Danes but neither woman budged even when the officer on the right glared at them in a menacing way.

"Where exactly do you think you're taking Miss Waterhouse?" Kat demanded, her blue eyes flashing. "And on what grounds?"

"Please step aside, Ma'am," said the officer on the left with mechanical courtesy. "We are simply fulfilling the orders on the papers we have just served to Miss Waterhouse. And we're taking her to the Human/Kindred Relations building for her claiming ceremony."

"Her what?" Sophia exclaimed, her green eyes wide with distress.

"Her claiming ceremony, where she will meet the Kindred warrior who has chosen her as a bride," the other officer explained patiently. "Miss Olivia Waterhouse has been drafted.

Read the rest of <u>Claimed</u> for free.

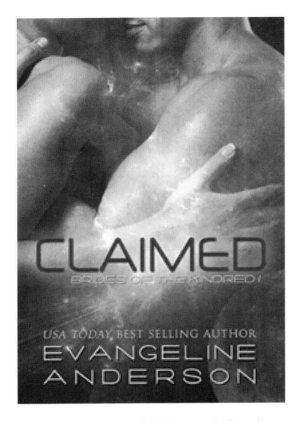

Read the rest of Claimed for free.

Also by Evangeline Anderson

Please note — these are Amazon/Kindle links. If you have a Nook or other reading device, please check my website for links to all other formats

Brides of the Kindred series

Claimed (Also available in Audio and Print format)

Hunted (Also available in Audio format)

Sought (Also Available in Audio format)
Found
Revealed
Pursued
Exiled
Shadowed
Chained
Divided
Devoured (Also available in Print)
Enhanced
Cursed
Enslaved
Targeted
Forgotten
Switched (coming 2016)
Mastering the Mistress (Brides of the Kindred Novella)

Born to Darkness series
Crimson Debt (Also available in Audio)
Scarlet Heat (Also available in Audio)
Ruby Shadows (Also available in Audio)
Cardinal Sins (Coming Soon)

Compendiums
Brides of the Kindred Volume One
Contains Claimed, Hunted, Sought and Found all in one volume
Born to Darkness Box Set
Contains Crimson Debt, Scarlet Heat, and Ruby Shadows all in one volume

Stand Alone Novels
The Institute: Daddy Issues (coming Feb 14, 2016)
Purity (Now available in Audio)
Stress Relief
The Last Man on Earth

YA Novels
The Academy

About the Author

Evangeline Anderson is the New York Times and USA Today Best Selling Author of the Brides of the Kindred and Born to Darkness series. She is thirty-something and lives in Florida with a husband, a son, and two cats. She had been writing erotic fiction for her own gratification for a number of years before it occurred to her to try and get paid for it. To her delight, she found that it was actually possible to get money for having a dirty mind and she has been writing paranormal and Sci-fi erotica steadily ever since.

You can find her online at her website www.evangelineanderson.com

Come visit for some free reads. Or, to be the first to find out about new books, join her newsletter.

Newsletter

Website
FaceBook
Twitter
Pinterest
Goodreads
Audio book newsletter.

Printed in Great Britain
by Amazon

68101070R00080